Murder at the Mansion

A Jessie Harper Paranormal Cozy Mystery
(Volume 3)

KJ Cornwall

Hendry Publishing

Contents

One

LIVERPOOL, 1930S

THE GRITTY SCENT OF salt and smoke wafted through the narrow streets of Liverpool, carrying tales of distant lands from the hulking freighters that adorned its docks.

Amidst the symphony of seagulls and the rhythmic clattering of cobblestones under the rush-hour traffic, a sense of anticipation hung in the air as if the city itself was holding its breath. Nestled amongst the city's time-worn limestone and sandstone edifices, a small office on Dale Street bore witness to this pulsating life. That office was the Dale Street Private Investigations Agency.

Behind its weathered oak desk sat Jessie Harper, her auburn hair knotted in stern practicality, her hazel eyes piercing through an intriguing article in the day's newspaper. The chaotic harmony of the city outside mirrored Jessie's own world - a whirlwind of case files and cryptic notes, each one a silent testament to her relentless pursuit of truth.

In the dimly lit room, the sweet scent of burning pipe tobacco filled the air, a testament to George Jenkin's habit. The crackling fire in the hearth cast dancing shadows on his weathered face, highlighting the deep lines etched by time and hardship.

His fingers traced the worn leather of his chair, a silent melody played out of familiarity. The rhythmic tapping of his cane against the wooden floor echoed in the silence, punctuating their conversation with an uncomfortable reminder of battles fought and won.

Across from him, Jessie, now in her early thirties and some ten years the man's junior watched intently, her gaze flickering between the man, his cane, and his pipe; her thoughts hidden behind a veil of polite interest. The tension hung heavy between them - a tangible force that threatened to consume the room.

Jessie glanced up from the article. "This missing jewel case has me stumped. All signs point to the husband, but there's no hard evidence."

George let out a sigh, smoke swirling around his head. "We'll crack it soon enough. We always do."

Jessie nodded, a determined look in her eyes. "Too right. We'll get to the bottom of this, one way or another."

The two exchanged a knowing look, their shared commitment to solving cases clear. They had built a reputation in Liverpool for their dogged pursuit of the truth.

The distant honking of car horns and the chatter of pedestrians drifted in through the window. Liverpool carried on around them, unaware of the pivotal role this unassuming first floor office on Dale Street played in keeping the city safe.

The door to the office burst open, the bell above it jangling loudly. Isabel, the receptionist hardly had chance to open her mouth when Lady Evelyn Montague swept past her, her face pale and eyes wide with fear. She clutched a stack of letters in her gloved hands.

"I'm sorry but I have no time for the usual formalities in waiting for your receptionist to announce my presence. I am Lady Evelyn Montague of Montague Mansion. Mr Jenkins, Miss Harper, you must help me!" she cried. "I'm being threatened, blackmailed!"

George set his pipe down calmly and leaned forward, gesturing to a chair. "Have a seat, Lady Montague. Tell us what's happened."

Lady Montague sank into the chair, crumpling the letters in her tight grip. "For weeks now I've been receiving the most dreadful letters. They say if I don't pay the blackmailer, harm will come to me and my family."

She thrust the papers toward them. Jessie took them and scanned the contents, her brow furrowing.

"The last letter said one of my relatives or a friend will be killed if I don't cooperate," Lady Montague continued, wringing a handkerchief in her hands. "You must find who's behind this before they make good on these horrible threats!" Through sobs, she managed to say, "Please excuse me. May I use your bathroom to compose myself. I feel such a helpless fool."

"I'll show you, my lady," Isabel said and left the office to show Lady Montague the bathroom just off the corridor.

As they were leaving, George met her panicked gaze evenly. "Don't you worry. We'll get to the bottom of this."

With Lady Montague gone, George leaned on his cane, standing up in one smooth motion despite his injury. "Jessie, let's start with interviewing the staff at Lady Montague's estate. There may be clues to this scoundrel's identity there."

Jessie was already planning the first steps. "Right. That makes sense. When she comes back, we need to ask her about any others who are residing at the mansion too such as family. We can rule no one out at this stage."

Five minutes later, Isabel escorted a now composed Lady Montague back into the office. Isabel took her leave and retired to the reception area.

George, ever the gentleman, proffered a seat for Lady Montague. Taking the seat, Lady Montague looked between them, relief washing over her features. "Oh, thank you both! I know I can rely on you to bring this villain to justice."

George gave her a reassuring pat on the shoulder. "No one threatens innocents in our city or its environs. We'll uncover the truth, have no doubt about that."

Jessie holding the letters, said. "We'll keep these for the time being as a closer examination may reveal some clues to the writer's identity. We will be in touch soon. I suggest you go home and be with your family. We're on the case now."

Lady Montague nodded. "Yes, I will, thank you."

"Before you go, besides your servants, who else is staying at the mansion?" Jessie said.

"It's my seventieth birthday. Today, in fact. Most of my family and friends are staying at the mansion to help me celebrate. Even my old friend, Professor Langford, the renowned archaeologist, and his assistant, Oscar, travelled from Egypt to help me celebrate. These threatening letters will ruin everything."

"So, quite the houseful... or should I say mansion full... pardon my sense of humour," George said.

Lady Evelyn smiled, "I like that in a man for two reasons. Firstly, it shows he is not some old fuddy duddy, and more importantly, it shows you will not stand on ceremony."

"Why, thank you." George said, "the latter is important in our line of work."

"There is still room at the mansion so I insist you both stay for the week. I will also put a study at your disposal as your temporary headquarters. Is that acceptable? Please, let me know if there is anything more I can provide to aid your investigation," Lady Montague continued earnestly. "I will open my home and my affairs to you completely. My staff are at your disposal as well."

"More than acceptable, my lady," Jessie said.

George rose from his chair, leaning on his cane for support. Despite the lingering pain from his war wound, he met Lady Montague's frightened gaze with a gentle smile.

"My lady, you have my word that we will do everything in our power to get to the bottom of these threats and keep you safe from harm. On my honour as a gentleman, no villain will lay a finger on you while you are in our care."

His voice was warm but firm, exuding a quiet confidence. Though he spoke softly, his eyes flashed with steely resolve. Lady Montague seemed to relax ever so slightly under the weight of his sincerity.

Meanwhile, Jessie had grabbed a fresh notebook and pen. With meticulous care, she neatly printed Lady Montague's name and the date at the top of the first page. Her mind was already churning with questions to ask and avenues to investigate. No detail would escape her notice; no lead would be left unfollowed. The truth was out there, and she would find it using her intellect, intuition, and uncompromising diligence.

"Some case notes before you leave us, if you don't mind, my lady," Jessie said and without waiting continued, "now then," she said briskly, "let's start from the beginning. When did you receive the first letter, and did you note anything peculiar about the envelope or handwriting?"

Pen poised, Jessie listened intently as Lady Montague began recounting the chain of sinister events. A fierce glint shone in Jessie's hazel eyes. The hunt for answers had begun.

Lady Montague gathered her skirts and hurried from the office, anxiety etched on her pale face. As soon as the door clicked shut behind her, Jessie and George exchanged a meaningful look.

"Well, this is quite the curious case," remarked George, leaning both hands on his cane as he pondered their new assignment.

Eager to begin, they moved briskly to gather coats and hats. Donning her favourite wool coat, Jessie felt a familiar thrill. A new case brought with it promise - of intrigue, justice but most of all adventure!

As Lady Montague hurried out of the office to her waiting driver and the Rolls Royce, Jessie and George exchanged a determined look. The thrill of a new mystery quickened their pulses, but even more so, their sense of duty compelled them. Someone needed their help, and they would answer the call.

Jessie smoothed back an errant auburn curl that had escaped from her tidy bun as she watched Lady Montague rush anxiously from their office. Though outwardly composed, Jessie's hazel eyes shone with steely determination. This new case ignited her unrelenting drive to uncover the truth and bring criminals to justice.

She turned to her partner. "Well George, it seems we have quite the mystery on our hands. Death threats and strange letters - clearly someone means Lady Montague harm."

George nodded, his face creased in thought. "Yes, a most distressing business. That poor woman was beside herself with fear." He leaned both hands on his cane, steadying his bad leg. Though injured in the war, nothing could diminish his resolve when people needed defending.

"We'd best pay a visit to Lady Montague's estate straight away," Jessie suggested briskly. "Perhaps examining the letters and interviewing her staff will yield some clues."

"Capital idea." George grinned, his eyes glinting with anticipation. "Let's be off, partner. Well, this is quite the curious case," remarked George, leaning both hands on his cane as he pondered their new assignment.

Jessie nodded. "Very sinister indeed. We must act swiftly but cautiously - lives could be at risk."

George hummed in agreement. "Let's start by examining the letters ourselves. I suspect they may contain clues about the sender that Lady Montague overlooked in her distress."

"An excellent thought," said Jessie approvingly. She was impressed by George's insight, as always. "We should also speak with the staff at Montague Mansion. Perhaps they noticed something suspicious before the letters arrived."

George smiled. "Quite right, quite right. Two heads are always better than one, eh Jessie?"

Jessie returned his smile. Their teamwork was seamless after many years working together. She knew they would unravel this mystery, same as all the rest.

George retrieved a magnifying glass from the top drawer of his desk then laid out the letters so he could examine the front and back of each letter checking for fingerprints.

"That is unusual," he said, "there is a total absence of fingerprints. Nary a smudge or a partial."

"Well," Khan said, "Perhaps like Lady Evelyn the writer wore gloves... or perhaps the writer wasn't human at all."

"The latter would certainly explain their absence but that is very scary," Jessie said. "Enough conjecture, let's go."

Eager to begin, they moved briskly to gather coats and hats. Jessie felt a familiar thrill. A new case brought with it promise - of intrigue, of justice, and of adventure most of all.

At her side, George adjusted his homburg and picked up his cane, looking every inch the seasoned investigator. But Jessie detected a sparkle of excitement in his eyes. However, many mysteries they solved, that sense of anticipation never faded.

"Don't forget me," a familiar feline voice said, "you will need my unique skills, no doubt," Khan added.

Aside from his observations about the lack of fingerprints on the letters, Khan had remained silent so far. He had also been silent and invisible throughout the exchange with Lady Montague as he must. Originally, he could only speak to and be heard by Jessie and now George as well. As time went by, Detective Sergeant Bill Roberts of the Liverpool City Police and a mentor to George and Jessie, could also hear Khan. No other humans could hear him. For a mystical cat, he also had the unpredictable supernatural ability to make himself invisible. Now that Lady Montague had left, Khan knew it was an opportune time to join Jessie and George in their new adventure.

Jessie turned to the mysterious feline, "Khan, do you have any insights for us?"

"Not yet, young ones, I will reserve judgement until I know more details."

First, Jessie and George packed small bags with a change of clothing anticipating a few nights stay at the mansion before together with Khan they strode out the door, minds racing with clues and speculation. Jessie had insisted she drive to Montague Manor in the Austin Seven, a symbol of the detective agency's success. It was parked a few hundred yards away in Tithebarn Street. George knew better than to argue about it.

Two

MONTAGUE MANSION

As Jessie and George stepped out onto the bustling streets of Liverpool, they were immersed in the vibrant atmosphere of the 1930s. Newsboys shouted the latest headlines as they waved newspapers. Motorcars rumbled past, dodging horse-drawn carriages, carts laden with goods, and double decker trams overflowing with passengers. Men in various styles of hats hurried along the pavement, briefcases in hand, as women in smart overcoats perused shop windows.

Jessie took a deep breath, inhaling the mingled scents of petrol fumes, roasting coffee, and hops from the nearby brewery, and the salty breeze coming off the River Mersey. Liverpool was a working city, industrious, and vibrant as well as energetic. As they made their way through the crowds, she felt invigorated by the familiar sights and sounds.

Beside her, George was scanning the busy street, looking for where Jessie had parked the car. Spotting it close to Liverpool Exchange railway station he raised his cane, pointing towards it. The gang of three, two humans and a magical black cat, climbed inside the saloon car.

"Montague Mansion, and quickly if you please," George joked with Jessie who was now behind the steering wheel. Settling back in his seat, he gave Jessie a knowing look. The game was on. Lady Montague was relying on them to uncover the source of the threats and they would not fail her.

Jessie met George's gaze with a determined nod. Whoever was behind the sinister letters, she and George would track them down. Justice would be served. Concentrating on the busy streets, Jessie steeled herself for the investigation ahead. The black Austin Seven carried them onwards, bringing them closer to the mystery awaiting them at Montague Mansion.

The car sped through the bustling streets of Liverpool, with Jessie weaving expertly between trams, buses, and pedestrians. George gazed out the window, watching the rows of brick townhouses and smoke-belching factories fly past in a blur. His mind raced with questions about Lady Montague and the death threats she had received. Who would want to harm the wealthy widow? And why send such chilling letters?

George smoked his pipe pensively, no doubt pondering the answers to these mysteries. Though he projected an air of calm, Jessie knew her partner's brilliant mind was already analysing the facts and forming hypotheses.

As the journey carried them farther from the city centre, the surroundings grew more rural. Tidy fields and quaint cottages replaced the crowded tenements and warehouses. Up ahead, Jessie spotted a wrought iron gate flanked by high stone walls - the entrance to the driveway of Montague Mansion.

Jessie drove the car through the imposing gates and continued up the tree-lined drive. In the distance, Montague Mansion came into view, an elegant Georgian mansion built of limestone. Jessie felt a thrill of anticipation. Somewhere within those walls lay the key to this sinister puzzle.

It was now mid-afternoon on an early December day and dusk was fast approaching. At the end of the long driveway, the looming silhouette of Montague Mansion pierced the night sky, The sprawling mansion loomed against the dusky sky, its stoic stone façade punctuated by windows that flickered with the warm glow of internal life yet betrayed nothing of the mysteries inside. Its sprawling wings disappearing into the darkness. Ivy crawled up the weathered stone walls like bony fingers grasping for a hold.

Inside, shadows danced across the marble floors as moonlight filtered through stained glass windows.

"Here we are," Jessie murmured, her gaze fixed on the towering turrets that reached for the heavens like silent sentinels. The mansion's grandeur was undeniable, a testament to a bygone era where opulence was etched into every brick and balustrade.

"Looks like something straight out of an Agatha Christie novel," George said, stepping out of the car, his hands shoved into the pockets of his overcoat.

"Or a Bram Stoker one," Jessie replied, the hairs on her arms standing up despite her attempt at humour. Khan leaped gracefully onto the gravel driveway, his black fur absorbing the twilight shadows that played around the manicured gardens.

"Ah, the perfect setting for a feline detective to make his mark," Khan chimed in, his tail swishing with anticipation. "The air is thick with secrets."

"Let's keep our wits about us," Jessie cautioned, locking the car with a turn of the key. "Remember, we're here to find answers, not to admire the architecture."

"Right you are," George agreed, adjusting his glasses. "Though I must admit, it does have a certain... ambience."

Together, they ascended the stone steps and rang the bell whilst Khan made himself invisible.

The huge oak entrance door of Lady Montague's mansion groaned open as if reluctant to reveal the secrets held within its ancient walls.

Three

LADY EVELYN MONTAGUE

A CANDLE FLICKERED IN the doorway, casting an amber glow on the figure who appeared. Lady Evelyn Montague swept into the cavernous foyer, the train of her emerald velvet dress whispering across the floor. Her salt and pepper hair was piled high atop her head, accented by a feathered fascinator tilted at a precarious angle.

"Welcome, do come in, I've been expecting you," she said, extending a gloved hand in greeting. Her voice was breathy and lilting, each word pronounced with purpose. She clasped her hands together and gave a little hop, her numerous jangling bracelets sliding down her thin wrists.

"We simply must get to the bottom of these mysterious happenings. The staff are convinced the manor is haunted, can you imagine?" She pressed a dramatic hand to her chest. "Me? Sharing my home with ghosts? Good heavens."

Jessie wasn't convinced by Lady Evelyn's attempt at belittling the thought of her home being haunted. A thought reinforced by their host's demeanour.

Lady Montague fluttered around the room, indicating various artefacts and furnishings. She paused to caress an antique vase, leaning in to examine it closely through her jewelled lorgnette.

"Now where did I put that blasted service bell? I've asked the housekeeper to prepare supper in the sitting room given the late hour. You will join me, won't you?" She looked up expectantly, awaiting their response.

Lady Montague's enthusiasm was met with polite smiles from Jessie Harper and George Jenkins as they entered the foyer. The owners of the Dale Street Private Investigations Agency were accustomed to eccentric clients, though Lady Montague's dramatic flair was amusement tinged with wariness.

Jessie tucked an errant auburn curl back into her neat chignon, while George ran a hand through his dark hair. Their eyes met in a wordless exchange - the opulence of the manor was intriguing, but they would reserve judgement on Lady Montague's claims until they had all the facts.

"A pleasure to meet you again so soon, Lady Montague," Jessie said smoothly. "Please, lead the way to the sitting room. We're happy to discuss your concerns over supper."

George nodded. "We'll keep an open mind as we investigate these... happenings, as you say. Our priority is getting to the truth."

Always open minded about ghosts, Jessie and George were professionals devoted to solving puzzles and mysteries. A manor with a reputation for being haunted was irresistible, ghost or not. Lady Montague's unconventional nature only added to the allure.

As they followed their hostess through the halls, Jessie made discreet notes in a small leather journal, while George keenly observed each room. Supper and an investigation into the unknown - an exciting prospect for the intrepid detectives.

Lady Montague led Jessie and George down a long, dimly lit hallway, her flowing emerald gown billowing behind her. She paused dramatically outside a set of large oak doors.

"Beyond these doors lies the scene of the most troubling events," she whispered. "I must warn you, once witnessed, the images cannot be erased."

Jessie and George exchanged a subtle glance. Theatrics aside, Lady Montague seemed genuinely distressed. This confirmed Jessie's earlier thoughts about Lady Evelyn's behaviour.

"We appreciate the concern, my lady," George said gently. "But we've seen our fair share of disturbing sights in this line of work. We'll proceed with open minds."

Lady Montague nodded, her expression grave. "Very well. But don't say I didn't warn you."

She pushed open the doors with a creak. Jessie and George stepped inside, surveying the room. It was a lavish sitting room, with fine antique furnishings and large bay windows that looked out over the misty grounds. Nothing seemed amiss.

"Over here," Lady Montague murmured, drifting toward the settee. "This is where I first saw it."

Jessie moved closer, scrutinising the area. The settee was tufted velvet, the sheen worn in places. Noting a faint discoloration on one cushion, she met George's eye knowingly. Evidence.

"And where exactly did you see...it?" George asked.

Lady Montague pointed a trembling finger. "Right there. A ghostly figure, hovering by the windows. Staring at me with hollow eyes!" She shuddered.

Jessie pulled a small pocket torch from her bag, leaning in to examine the cushion further. The plot thickens, she thought, stifling a smile.

Jessie straightened up, casting her gaze around the room once more. There had to be some logical explanation for Lady Montague's supposed spectral visitor. Perhaps a draft from the windows was playing tricks, casting odd shadows. Or fatigue and imagination had conjured the phantom. They would need to investigate further.

"When did you first experience this...sighting?" George asked, notebook in hand.

Lady Montague smoothed her dress. "Just over a fortnight ago. I'd fallen asleep here after dinner and awoke to find it lurking." She shivered. "Ghastly business."

Jessie's eyes narrowed thoughtfully. "And it's appeared since then?"

"Oh yes, several times." Lady Montague nodded. "Always here in the sitting room, in the dead of night."

"Hmm." George scribbled some notes. "No other odd occurrences? Strange sounds, objects moving?"

Lady Montague considered this. "Well, the servants have mentioned the candles flickering unexpectedly. And feeling sudden chills in the hallway." She leaned forward. "Mark my words, this place is haunted!"

Jessie and George exchanged a look. More likely, they had a mortal intruder using tricks and illusions. But they would need solid evidence before making accusations.

"We'll be here tonight when it appears," Jessie said. "Set up a camera with a flash bulb and monitor for any suspicious activity."

Lady Montague clasped her hands. "Oh, bless you! I knew I could count on the Dale Street detectives to solve this mystery."

Jessie smiled. The game was on. With their wits and experience, no phantom could elude them for long.

Jessie and George spent the next few hours preparing for their overnight vigil at Lady Montague's mansion. They positioned the camera on a stand in the sitting room, setting the lens aperture for the flash bulb exposure. They also placed a rather bulky microphone in the hallway. When sound activated, it would relay to a dynamic loudspeaker so Jessie and George could hear the sounds.

Donning dark clothing, they took up positions out of sight but with a clear view of the sitting room. The only sounds were the ticking of a grandfather clock and occasional creaks and groans as the old house settled.

As midnight approached, Jessie and George grew alert, senses primed for any odd occurrences. The room remained still and empty, moonlight casting a pale glow across the floor.

"No activity yet," Jessie whispered. "But it's early."

George nodded, eyes scanning the room. "We may be in for a long wait-"

He halted as a loud thump echoed from upstairs, followed by a drawn-out scraping noise. The detectives tensed, exchanging a meaningful look.

"The game's afoot," Jessie murmured, quickly checking the time. "Let's investigate."

Moving swiftly, they ascended the grand staircase, senses tingling with anticipation. This is what they lived for - the thrill of the hunt. The phantom was about to meet its match.

Jessie and George reached the top of the grand staircase, eyes and ears alert for any sign of the phantom. Moonlight filtered in through tall, mullioned windows, casting an eerie glow across the hallway. Ancient portraits and tapestries lined the walls, their occupants seeming to watch the detectives' every move.

At the end of the hall stood an imposing set of double doors. As Jessie and George approached cautiously, another thump sounded from behind the doors, followed by a long, low moan.

Exchanging quizzical glances, Jessie grasped the ornate door handle and turned it slowly. The door creaked open to reveal a spacious bedchamber draped in shadows. A four-poster canopy bed dominated the room, its velvet curtains partially drawn.

With no warning, the curtains fluttered as if stirred by an unseen hand. A pale, wispy shape began to materialise next to the bed, slowly taking on the form of a woman in a flowing nightgown. Her eyes were hollow, her skin like parchment. She opened her mouth in a soundless wail.

Jessie and George stood transfixed, scarcely believing the sight before them. Then the phantom began gliding toward them, her bony hands outstretched.

Snapping out of their shock, the detectives leapt into action. Jessie whipped out her patented spiritual disruption device while George grabbed an iron fire poker. Time to send this spook back where it came from.

Then... as soon as it appeared... it was gone.

Four

A Dead Body

"Blasted camera, it is far too big and clumsy to lug around. It's as if that ghost knew the camera and recording device were set up in a different room," George said.

"And where's Khan when you need him," Jessie said.

George and Jessie's thoughts were interrupted when at the far side of the room, a door creaked open, revealing a dimly lit study. Jessie and George approached the door as it slammed shut.

"Blast! Now what do we do?" George said.

"Use this," Jessie said, fishing in her bag for the skeleton key Lady Evelyn had entrusted to her as an aid in their investigations.

Jessie stepped inside, her keen eyes scanning the room. The curtains were drawn, casting shadows across the Persian rug and mahogany desk.

"No signs of forced entry," murmured George as he first examined the door then the locked windows.

Jessie nodded, noting the seeming peculiar lack of disturbance. But then she saw the giant globe in the corner, strangely askew on its axis.

"Rather odd, isn't it?" she mused. "It seems everything is perfectly in place, except..."

George crossed to the desk, trailing a finger through the thin layer of dust. "Untouched for days, I'd wager."

He paused, frowning at the antique silver letter opener lying atop a stack of unopened post. Jessie's thoughts mirrored his own. Why leave such a convenient weapon unused?

Kneeling, Jessie spotted a faint scuff mark marring the intricate floral pattern of the rug. She brushed her fingers over the fibres. The abrasion felt fresh.

"A slip of the heel, perhaps a tussle," she murmured. George raised an eyebrow.

"With nary a paper out of place? Singularly perplexing."

Jessie stood, adjusting the magnifying glass hanging from her neck. There was much yet to unravel in this seemingly impossible locked room mystery. But her mind churned with clues, and she relished the challenge ahead.

Jessie's gaze landed on the imposing mahogany desk, its surface bare except for a leather blotter and an ornate inkstand. Behind it sat a high-backed chair, turned at an odd angle away from the desk.

She circled around, intent on examining the chair. But as it swivelled into view, she stumbled back with a gasp.

"Good heavens!"

Sprawled across the seat was the body of Professor Langford, his head lolled back at an unnatural angle. It appeared his neck had been broken. His skin had taken on a waxy pallor and his eyes were frozen open, staring vacantly past Jessie through wire-rimmed spectacles.

George rushed over. "Dead for some time, I'd say." He pressed two fingers to the Professor's neck, shaking his head grimly. "Neck snapped in two like a twig, that must have taken some strength."

Jessie suppressed a shudder, moving closer. Her shock quickly turned to intrigue as her gaze snagged on a strange pendant hanging around the corpse's neck. A silver amulet embossed with cryptic symbols.

"Now what have we here..." she murmured. Gingerly lifting the amulet between gloved fingers, she scrutinised the intricate carvings. A chill rippled through her.

"George, do you know what this is?"

He leaned in, brow furrowing. "Can't say I've seen the like before. But the markings suggest an occult origin."

Jessie released the amulet, mind racing. What secrets did this talisman hold? And what part had it played in the professor's bizarre demise? She had a nagging feeling the truth was far stranger than either could imagine. The game was truly afoot.

"A locked room murder is perplexing enough," Jessie mused aloud as she paced the study, "but an occult amulet takes this to a new level."

George nodded, scrutinising the room. "No signs of forced entry or struggle. All windows locked from inside. I'm sure the door was locked when we arrived. That must be right otherwise we wouldn't have required the skeleton key. But what about the door creaking and appearing to be ajar?" He gestured in frustration. "How does one manage such a feat?"

Just then, a haughty meow sounded from the doorway as Khan sauntered into the study. "Help me out here, Khan, what do you think?"

After a pause for thought, Khan said, "A common occurrence when a poltergeist or vengeful spirit wants to draw attention to his devilish wrongdoings."

"What? So, the spirit made us think we saw a door ajar and it creaked?" George said incredulously.

"Precisely," the wise cat said. "It wanted you to find the body."

Jessie paused before the body, gazing thoughtfully at the victim. "Perhaps this Professor Langford was more than he seemed. Could he have used this amulet to... transport himself somehow, only to meet his end here?"

"Intriguing theory," George said, stroking his chin. "Though we'd need more evidence to support something so fantastical."

"Amulet, you say. I believe I can shed some light on this peculiar artefact." Khan's green eyes glinted knowingly.

Jessie raised an eyebrow. "Well don't keep us in suspense, O Wise One. What do you know of this amulet?"

The cat sniffed, curling his tail. "I have lived many lives and seen many strange things, my dear. That particular amulet has a long, dark history. Some say it allows the wearer to walk between worlds. But there is always a price for such unnatural power." His gaze turned grim. "I suspect this professor has paid that price in full."

The amulet was silver, shaped like a five-pointed star and engraved with unfamiliar symbols. A large purple gemstone glittered at its centre. Jessie leant in closer to examine the amulet, noting the intricate symbols etched into the silver pendant. The metal felt cold and heavy in her hand, and she swore she could feel a faint pulse coming from within, like a heartbeat.

"Look here," she murmured, tracing her fingers along the edges. "These markings appear Sumerian, or perhaps

Babylonian. This central symbol resembles an ancient god..."

George peered over her shoulder. "Astute observation. The craftsmanship is remarkable. I'd wager this dates back thousands of years."

Khan sauntered closer, tail swishing back and forth. "An ancient and wicked thing. Meant to be locked away, not worn as a trinket." The cat's fur bristled as his gaze fixed on the amulet.

Jessie carefully placed the pendant and the amulet in an evidence bag which she then put into her satchel. "If this amulet is responsible for the professor's impossible murder, how was the deed done exactly?"

George paced the room, scrutinising every detail. He paused at the grand mahogany desk, noting the scattered papers and open books. "Perhaps he was studying the artefact? Trying to unlock its secrets?"

Khan jumped atop the desk, sniffing at the open texts. "Tampering with forces beyond his comprehension. The fool."

Jessie moved to the bookshelves, scanning the titles. Her fingers traced across leather-bound spines embossed with occult symbols. "Looks like Langford had quite the collection of arcane lore. But was he killed for his research, or by it?"

The three continued searching for any clue to explain how a man could be murdered in a locked room. But the more they uncovered about Professor Langford and his sinister amulet, the deeper the mystery became.

Jessie and George made their way downstairs to the grand foyer where Lady Evelyn and the other guests were gathered. Khan padded along behind them, his tail swishing with intrigue, invisible once more now.

Lady Evelyn greeted them anxiously. "Did you find anything? Please tell me you have some idea what happened to poor Professor Langford."

Jessie offered an empathetic smile. "We're still piecing things together, but we have a few questions that may help. What can you tell us about the professor's recent activities and acquaintances?"

Lady Evelyn waved them over to a settee and rang for tea. As they settled in, the other guests murmured quietly amongst themselves, stealing curious glances at Jessie and George.

"Let's see..." Lady Evelyn began slowly. "Arthur was a scholar and something of a recluse. He'd been obsessed with that dreadful amulet for months now. I did warn him dabbling in such things never led anywhere good. I asked Oscar, his assistant, to reinforce the warning but he flat refused saying the professor knows what he was doing.""

Jessie's hazel eyes narrowed with interest. "This amulet - did he say where he acquired it?"

"An artefact dealer in London, I believe. Though I never saw the wretched thing until..." Lady Evelyn dabbed at her eyes with a lace handkerchief.

George pulled out a small notebook, scribbling down details. "And had he made any breakthroughs recently? Did he confide in you about the amulet's meaning or purpose?"

Lady Evelyn shook her head. "I'm afraid he was quite secretive about the whole affair. But Oscar, his research assistant, may know more. He is probably at the village public house but I can send for him."

As Lady Evelyn gave instructions to a maid, Jessie surveyed the other guests. Some were elderly academics, some were family, but one young woman stood apart, staring out a window with a troubled expression.

Jessie's intuition prickled. There was more here than met the eye. She just needed to discern the subtle clues that would unravel this mystery.

"Jessie, once the assistant is found, please speak to Oscar and see what he knows. I will return to the crime scene." George knew Khan would follow.

George paced the room, with Khan in tow, brow furrowed in concentration as he examined the scene.

"The door was locked from the inside. We know that because when Jessie used the skeleton key, it dislodged the original key causing it to fall inside the room. There were no signs of forced entry," he mused. "The windows were latched as well. So how did the killer get in and out of a first-floor study?"

He paused by the desk, inspecting the scattered papers and books. "The professor was clearly searching for something before he died. But what?"

George's keen analytical mind pieced together the puzzle. "The amulet - it must be the key! He discovered something about its powers that someone wanted to keep hidden."

Just then, Khan leaped gracefully onto the desk, his green eyes unblinking. Jessie had now joined up with George and Khan.

"Beware the gems of Merlin," Khan intoned mysteriously. "Dark forces seek to possess their power."

Jessie and George exchanged a glance. Khan's prophecies always held truth if one could decipher them.

"Merlin..." Jessie murmured. "Then the amulet has origins in Arthurian legend?"

Khan flicked his tail. "Seek the Lady of the Lake, and you will find answers."

George jotted this down eagerly. "The Lady of the Lake...of course! She bestowed Excalibur onto King Arthur. This amulet must have come from her as well."

"We're on the right track," Jessie said decisively. The puzzle was coming together, piece by piece. All they needed now was concrete proof.

Jessie's hazel eyes shone with determination as she surveyed the room. "We need to uncover everything we can about this amulet. Its history, its powers - any detail may be important."

George nodded, his angular face set in concentration. "You're right. Let's comb this room again for any notes or books related to the amulet."

The pair set to work searching the cluttered office, sifting through the haphazard piles of parchments and strange artefacts. Jessie paused as her gaze fell on an ancient leather-bound tome tucked halfway under a stool.

"Here," she called to George, carefully extracting the book. "This looks promising."

George crossed over to peer at the faded gold lettering on the cover. "The Legends of Avalon," he read aloud. "This could be just what we need."

Jessie gently cracked open the book, the old pages crackling. Intricate illustrations and hand-lettered text in swirling calligraphy filled the yellowed parchment.

"This mentions the Lady of the Lake, the sword in the stone and gemstones with magical properties," Jessie murmured excitedly, scanning the pages. She came to a detailed drawing of a pendant. "Look, this amulet is nearly identical to the one we found on the professor!"

George's sharp eyes darted over the accompanying text. "You're right, this is key. We need to study this closely."

Khan peered over Jessie's shoulder, his green gaze intense. "The path ahead is fraught with peril; there is an intermingling here with Arthurian legend and ancient Egyptian lore... a dangerous combination," he warned ominously. "But justice must prevail."

Jessie stroked the cat's head. "Don't worry, we'll get to the bottom of this. No matter what the danger."

George tucked the book carefully into his satchel. "Let's get back and pore over every detail."

The trio hurried from the room, determined to decipher the secrets of the amulet and solve the confounding mystery.

Five

THE GHOST ORCHID

BACK IN THE MAKESHIFT office in the mansion, Jessie leaned back in the study chair, staring pensively at the crime scene photos spread across her desk.

The local constabulary had left copies for them but only after Lady Montague had insisted Jessie and George must conduct the investigation into the murder as they were already investigating the threatening letters.

The lady of the house had telephoned the Chief Constable of Lancashire to ensure 'her sleuths,' as she called them, be given a free reign. Unbeknown to Lady Montague, the chief had contacted Detective Sergeant Bill Roberts of the Liverpool City Police who gave the pair a glowing reference.

Jessie continued to examine the photographs... a gruesome tableau, but it only strengthened her resolve to catch the killer.

"Another senseless murder," she murmured.

George looked up from his own desk, stacked precariously with case files and books. "We'll get to the bottom of this one too," he said. His voice held steady conviction despite the late hour.

Jessie gave him a tired smile. They had been partners for years now, ever since she had left the library for a life of solving supernatural crimes. George matched her dedication to the work, even when the cases seemed unsolvable.

"The modus operandi doesn't match any of our previous cases," Jessie said, shuffling through the photos again. "No clear connections to the occult either."

"You think this might be related to the threats against Lady Evelyn?" George asked.

Jessie tapped a finger against her chin. "Could be. Hard to ignore the timing. Lady Evelyn's always had enemies, but these latest threats felt more serious."

George nodded. "If someone wanted to send a message, this murder would certainly do it. The professor was a close friend of hers."

"And killed in such a brutal way, in his own locked study," Jessie mused. She stood, walking over to the corkboard on the wall. It was filled with their notes on the case so far. "We're missing something..."

George joined her in front of the board, arms crossed. "The motive is key here. If we figure out why the killer wanted the professor dead, I think this whole case will unravel."

Jessie turned to him, eyes alight. "Where should we start digging first then?"

George smiled. "I'll put on a fresh pot of coffee."

Jessie's gaze landed on the paper bag sitting on her desk. Inside was the strange amulet found clutched in Professor Langford's hand. She picked it up, holding it closer to the light.

The amulet was silver, shaped like a five-pointed star and engraved with unfamiliar symbols. A large purple gemstone glittered at its centre.

"What do you make of this?" she asked George.

He stepped closer, scrutinising the artefact. "Definitely odd. Any ideas on the meaning behind those symbols?"

Jessie shook her head. "They don't match any languages or occult symbols I'm familiar with."

She crossed the room to one of the bookshelves, scanning the titles before selecting a heavy leather-bound tome.

"This might help provide some insight," she said, opening the book on her desk. George joined her as she flipped through the pages. "It's an encyclopaedia of magical artefacts throughout history."

The two pored over the book, looking for anything like the amulet. After several minutes, Jessie tapped a page excitedly.

"Here! This talks about protective amulets used by ancient cults. They were thought to ward off evil spirits." She traced a finger over the accompanying drawing, nearly identical to the one they had found.

"Protective?" George said. "So was the professor trying to protect himself from something?"

Jessie met his gaze. "Or someone..."

"So, what about Khan's mutterings about the Lady of the Lake and Arthurian legends?"

"Let's keep an open mind. He may be wrong but he is often right," Jessie said.

"Time to interview some staff, me thinks. Shall we start with the gardener?" George said.

Jessie and George stepped out into the hazy afternoon light, the amulet safely tucked away in an evidence bag in a locked drawer in their temporary office. Their first stop was to interview the gardener, Mr Thompson, who had raised the alarm on discovering the untouched supper tray outside the professor's room that morning.

They found him tending to the rose bushes along the front walkway. He was a slender man in his early sixties, with wispy grey hair peeking out from under his wide-brimmed hat. Though slender, he appeared strong and healthy no doubt because of his outdoor life.

"Mr Thompson, we're Jessie and George with the detective agency," Jessie said gently. "We just have a few questions about this morning. As I'm sure you know, the housekeeper called us to gain entry to the professor's room after you had told her about the supper tray."

The gardener looked up, his face pale. "Oh yes, dreadful business, that," he said, taking off his gloves. "Don't know who would want to hurt the poor professor."

George took out his notebook. "When exactly did you inform the housekeeper?"

"Who me? I told the housekeeper I found his supper tray still outside his study and that was most unusual."

"Okay, tell us what happened then." George said.

"First thing when I arrived, about half six, I unlocked the side door of that wing and went to check the corridors where the guests sleep like I always do." The gardener shuddered. "Quite a fright it gave me, when I heard the professor had been killed."

"Why? You don't appear to be easily frightened," Jessie said.

"Heard the mansion is haunted, miss. That's all."

"Did you notice anything else out of the ordinary?" Jessie asked. "Maybe sounds in the night, unfamiliar vehicles?"

Thompson shook his head. "Afraid not, miss. But I don't live on the grounds, just come in days to tend to the gardens. I kind of do a security check when I get here. Her ladyship pays me a bit extra to do that. "

They asked a few more questions, but it was clear the gardener could provide little help. As they turned to leave, Jessie had one last thought.

"Those lovely roses - did Professor Langford enjoy gardening as well?"

"Oh, heavens no," Thompson chuckled. "He hadn't a clue about plants. Lady Evelyn is the one with the green fingers in this family."

Jessie and George exchanged a look. That may be one more connection between the murder and the recent threats. Their next stop was the manor to speak with Lady Evelyn directly.

"Lady Evelyn, thank you for seeing us again so soon," Jessie said gently. "We know this is a difficult time."

Evelyn nodded, twisting a handkerchief between her fingers. "Yes, well, I want to help in any way I can. Poor Arthur..." Her voice trailed off.

George stepped forward. "We just spoke with your gardener and were intrigued to learn you are the one responsible for the lovely roses on the estate."

"Oh, yes." Evelyn seemed surprised by the change of subject. "Gardening has always been a passion of mine."

"It seems you and the professor had that in common," Jessie said. "We heard he recently imported a rare specimen all the way from South America."

Evelyn's eyes widened briefly. "I - I'm not sure-"

Jessie pressed on. "A Ghost Orchid, wasn't it? Quite a find."

The lady looked between them, distress evident on her face. When she spoke, her voice was barely a whisper. "I didn't want any of this to happen, you must believe me. But that orchid... Professor Langford wouldn't listen when I begged him to get rid of it. He had no idea what forces he was meddling with."

Jessie and George exchanged a startled glance. This was clearly a major development in the case. Lady Evelyn knew far more than she had revealed about the mysterious threats and Langford's disturbing demise.

Jessie leaned forward, her eyes bright with curiosity. "Lady Evelyn, I think it's time you told us everything you know about this orchid and your friend's death."

Lady Evelyn wrung her hands, glancing anxiously at the study door as if afraid they might be overheard. "I warned Arthur not to bring that wretched thing into my home. There were rumours, you see... legends that it was cursed." She shivered. "They say the orchid came from an ancient burial ground and that terrible things happen to those who try to possess it."

George furrowed his brow sceptically. "Cursed orchids and spooky legends? Forgive me, Lady Evelyn, but that seems a rather fantastical explanation for a man's murder."

"I know how it sounds!" Lady Evelyn cried. "I didn't want to believe it either. But Arthur was obsessed with adding the rarest specimens to his collection. When he finally acquired the Ghost Orchid, strange things started happening straight away."

"What sort of strange things?" Jessie asked gently.

"Noises in the night, objects moving on their own. And there were the notes warning him to get rid of the orchid, growing more threatening by the day. When he refused, the accidents started. Tripping on the stairs, nearly falling off a ladder in the garden. It was the curse, I just know it!" Lady Evelyn twisted the handkerchief fiercely. "On the day he... he died, we had a terrible row about it. I begged him one last time to be rid of the wretched plant. He just wouldn't listen!"

Jessie and George shared a look. This certainly put a new spin on things. Could there truly be a supernatural force at work? Or was the lady merely grasping at superstition to explain her friend's tragic end? They needed more facts...

"Where is the orchid now?" Jessie asked.

Lady Evelyn shuddered. "Locked away in the conservatory. I can't bear to even look at it. Please, you must get it out of here before the curse takes hold of this house completely!"

Jessie and George left Lady Evelyn's parlour with more questions than answers. As they walked down the oak-panelled hallway, Jessie shook her head.

"A cursed orchid? It seems a bit far-fetched, don't you think?"

George nodded, his brow furrowed in thought. "Far-fetched, yes, but we can't rule it out completely. Not when lives are at stake."

They had nearly reached the front door when a blood-curdling scream pierced the air. Jessie and George exchanged an alarmed look before racing up the grand staircase, following the echoes of panic.

Bursting into the upstairs gallery, they skidded to a halt. Lady Evelyn stood rigid, one hand pressed over her heart, the other pointing a trembling finger at an ornate wall mirror.

Scrawled across the glass in dripping red letters was a chilling message:

GET OUT OR YOU'RE NEXT

Jessie rushed to Lady Evelyn's side, gripping her arm in support. "My lady, are you alright?"

Lady Evelyn could only nod mutely, eyes fixed on the ominous warning.

George peered closely at the mirror. "It's not blood, just paint of some kind." He scratched at one of the letters with his fingernail and it smudged slightly.

"A vicious prank, meant to terrorise," Jessie said grimly. She turned to Lady Evelyn. "You're not safe here. Let us take you somewhere secure while we get to the bottom of this."

Lady Evelyn opened her mouth to reply when a shrill ring pierced the air. Jessie picked up the nearby ringing telephone but heard nothing.

"Crank call," she murmured. "Shall I answer?"

George nodded. "Yes, better had."

"Hello?" Jessie said.

She heard a crackling recording of a man's voice:

"Beware the ghost orchid's curse. All who possess it shall face a fate far worse..."

The call ended abruptly. Jessie relayed the message to George and Lady Montague.

Lady Evelyn swayed on her feet. "It's the curse! It's coming for me next!"

Jessie caught the lady's arm, exchanging a worried look with George. This case had just taken a chilling turn into the realm of the paranormal. And lives hung in the balance.

Six

THE INVESTIGATION IS UNDERWAY

JESSIE LEANED BACK IN the office chair, and tempted to prop her feet up on the antique desk in the makeshift headquarters but she would not dare nor do that. Such lack of manners were not her style. "So, Lady Evelyn's relatives. What do we know so far?"

George glanced up from organising a stack of notes. "Not much, unfortunately. Other than they're supposedly the heirs to her considerable estate. But Baxter, the lawyer can help us with that side of things."

Khan leapt up onto the desk, his tail swishing as he batted at a stray paperclip. "Yes, a greedy, secretive bunch by all accounts." He looked up, his green eyes glinting knowingly. "We'll need to observe them closely during the interviews."

Jessie nodded, folding her arms. "Agreed. Their behaviour and interactions with each other could reveal potential motives or conflicts."

A knock at the door interrupted their discussion. Jessie raised an eyebrow at George as she rose to answer it.

She opened the door to find a small crowd gathered outside and instructed to do so by Lady Evelyn herself. Her ladyship's relatives had arrived, eyeing Jessie and George with unveiled suspicion.

"Welcome, please come in," Jessie said briskly, beckoning them inside and ignoring the indifference emanating from the crowd.

First came Lady Evelyn's cousin Nigel, a portly man perspiring heavily in an ill-fitting suit, along with his nervous wife Fiona. Next, her flashy niece Violet swaggered in, dripping in jewels, with her much older husband Walter in tow. Finally, Bartholomew, another of Lady Evelyn's cousins slinked in, his eyes shifty and his smile unctuous.

Jessie studied them closely as George made introductions. Their whispered conversations and sideways glances revealed their unease. Khan's tail twitched from his perch atop the desk, his gaze fixed on the relatives, as if to say the game was afoot and not liking what he saw.

Jessie nodded to George, who began ushering the relatives into separate rooms for their interviews.

First was Nigel, Lady Evelyn's rotund cousin. He mopped his brow with a monogrammed handkerchief as he settled into the chair across from Jessie.

"So, Nigel, tell me about your relationship with Lady Evelyn," Jessie began gently.

Nigel shifted in his seat. "Oh, we were quite close as children. But we grew apart as adults, you know how it goes."

Jessie studied his face. His eyes kept darting around the room, landing on the antique vases and ornate lamps.

"And were you in contact recently?" Jessie asked.

"Here and there," Nigel said vaguely, "and then the invitation to her birthday bash. I was quite surprised."

Jessie leaned forward. "Nigel, if you know anything that could help us, it's best to be forthright."

He wrung his hands. "Well, I may have asked Evie for a small loan last month. My business hasn't been doing well, you see."

"I see. And did she oblige?"

Nigel flushed. "She refused in no uncertain terms. Said I needed to learn to manage my finances. It caused quite a row between us."

Jessie nodded, noting his potential motive. Financial trouble paired with rejection was a combustible mix.

Meanwhile, in the next room, George was speaking with Mr Baxter, Lady Evelyn's lawyer. The man sat ramrod straight, his eyes flinty behind wire-rimmed spectacles. His lips were pursed in a thin line.

"How long have you worked for Lady Montague?" George asked politely.

"Over a decade," Baxter said crisply. "I handle all her legal and financial affairs."

George studied the man's rigid demeanour and evasive eyes. He would not give information freely. This called for a subtle approach.

"She must have relied on you greatly," George said. "Handling that kind of responsibility for so long builds an immense trust."

Baxter's expression flickered almost imperceptibly. "Yes, Lady Montague trusts me fully," he said quietly.

George nodded. "Then you must want to see justice done for her as much as we do."

Baxter cleared his throat, looking away. "I simply hope you find whoever is responsible for sending those ghastly threats and are swift at finding the professor's killer, of course."

George suppressed a smile. The lawyer was clearly hiding something. It was only a matter of time until they uncovered the truth.

George and Jessie retreated to their makeshift office when they heard another knock on the door. Jessie opened the door but initially saw no one. Then, as if hiding, the maid Abigail emerged from the shadows of the hallway, the soft light casting an eerie glow on her pale face. Her eyes shifted nervously as she wrung her hands on her apron.

"I am instructed to inform you that the guests and other members of her ladyship's family are at your disposal in the ballroom," she murmured, before disappearing back down the dark corridor.

Jessie and George exchanged a glance. It was time to meet the remainder of the family and the eccentric friends Lady Evelyn had surrounded herself with in her later years and who had also been invited to the birthday bash.

As George and Jessie waited, the grand ballroom doors flung open and in burst Priscilla Heatherington, wearing a flamboyant hat with peacock feathers. On her arm was Lord Ambrose Whittington, waving a jewelled cane and wearing a patched velvet coat. Behind them trailed Dame Olivia Rosemont, her face caked in heavy makeup and dressed in ruffles and frills.

"Oh darling, this is simply dreadful!" cried Priscilla, fanning herself dramatically.

"Quite dreadful indeed," murmured Ambrose.

"Our poor Evelyn!" wailed Olivia. "Who could have done something so ghastly as sending death threats?"

"And the professor's murder, of course," Priscilla added.

Jessie studied the trio carefully. They were certainly eccentric and bizarre in their attire and mannerisms. But were they hiding something more sinister beneath the flamboyance? She would need to probe deeper to find out.

For now, their arrival added a touch of the absurd to an already mystifying situation. Jessie suppressed a smile as Khan leapt up and batted at one of Priscilla's dangling feathers, providing a moment of lightness in the heavy atmosphere.

They still had much to unravel in this mystery. But at least they had been introduced to some of the key players within Montague Mansion, friends, relatives of Lady Evelyn, her lawyer and of course, her servants. The truth waited silently within these walls, waiting to be brought into the light.

Jessie's gaze moved to George as he approached the small gathering of relatives huddled in the corner of the ballroom, whispering among themselves. She knew George would use his easy charm and friendly demeanour to try and glean some information from them.

"Good day, I'm George Jenkins, as you know Lady Evelyn has hired us to investigate the death threats made against her and the murder of Professor Langford," he said warmly, extending his hand. The relatives eyed him suspiciously before one finally shook his hand and introduced himself as Edmund Montague, Evelyn's nephew.

"Terrible business, this whole affair," George remarked conversationally. "We want to get to the bottom of it, for Lady Evelyn's sake."

Edmund nodded. "Yes, Aunt Evelyn is a fine woman. It's a shame what's happened." His eyes darted around nervously.

"You must be close to her," George said. "Any idea who could have wanted to cause her harm?"

Edmund fidgeted with his cufflinks. "No, no, can't imagine who would do this..." His voice trailed off evasively.

Jessie watched the exchange intently. George was keeping his tone light and casual, but she could tell he sensed Edmund was holding something back. There was more to uncover about these relatives and their potential motives.

She caught George's eye discreetly from across the room. A look passed between them, acknowledging they were on the right track. They hoped the pieces of this mystery were slowly coming together.

Khan's ears perked up as he slipped away unseen from the tense gathering. His whiskers twitched eagerly as he sniffed along the hallway's ornate wallpaper, the scent of secrets drawing him onwards. His paws silently padded up a winding staircase, past faded portraits whose eyes seemed to follow the prowling feline. Khan paused, detecting a whisper of air from behind an ancient tapestry. Pushing past it revealed a narrow passage, shrouded in cobwebs.

The cat's eyes glowed knowingly. His sleek figure disappeared into the darkness, intent on uncovering what these walls had hidden for decades. Dusty bookshelves, locked trunks, and the echoes of the past awaited discovery in this labyrinth of buried truth.

Khan was certain this mansion held the key to Lady Evelyn's fate. He needed only follow his feline instincts to unravel each thread. Jessie and George may question the friends and relatives, but Khan would interrogate the house itself. Its secrets now stirred, emerging from the shadows at the prodding of his paws.

On spotting the maid in a corner of the ballroom, George approached Abigail discreetly, noticing how the maid's eyes shifted around the room warily.

"Abigail, a word if you please," George said politely.

The maid nodded hesitantly. George led her to a quiet annexe just off the ballroom.

"I understand you are very close to Lady Evelyn," George began gently. "We only want to find out who might have wanted to harm her... threaten her. Anything you can tell us would be a great help."

Abigail bit her lip. "I don't know anything," she said unconvincingly.

George raised an eyebrow. "Now Abigail, I can tell you're holding something back. Your loyalty to Lady Evelyn or someone else in the mansion is admirable, but if you know something, it could prove vital to our investigation."

The maid wrung her hands, conflicted. Finally, she leaned in and whispered. "The night before the professor's murder, I saw Mr Baxter, her lawyer, arguing heatedly with her. He seemed quite upset when he left."

George's eyes widened. This could be a promising lead. "Thank you, Abigail, your discretion is appreciated. We'll look further into Mr Baxter."

The maid nodded before slipping away nervously.

Across the ballroom, Jessie caught George's eye, having deduced he had just held a conversation with Abigail. Another piece of the puzzle had fallen into place. Lady Evelyn's inner circle held secrets that might explain her fate.

Jessie felt they were closing in on the truth. But motives and alibis would need to be confirmed. They had potential suspects now, but not yet definitive answers. She and George exchanged a knowing look - the hunt was on.

Jessie and George retreated to their makeshift office, a study tucked away on the mansion's first floor. Khan leapt up onto the desk, his tail swishing as he eyed them expectantly.

"Well, that was certainly an intriguing introduction to our cast of characters," Jessie said wryly, scratching the cat behind his ears.

George nodded. "Quite the collection of eccentric relatives and associates. But I believe we've uncovered some promising leads."

He recounted the details of his discussion with the nervous maid Abigail, and her revelation about the argument between Lady Evelyn and Mr Baxter.

"There's definitely more to that story," Jessie agreed. "We'll need to investigate Baxter thoroughly, along with all the relatives angling for a piece of her estate."

Khan meowed loudly as if in agreement. Jessie smiled and continued petting the observant feline.

"Of course, we can't rule out the possibility of other unknown players in this mystery," George added thoughtfully. "Lady Evelyn's life may hold many secrets we've yet to uncover."

Jessie's eyes shone with determination. "Then we'll just have to keep digging. These walls hold the answers - I can feel it."

Their scheming was suddenly interrupted by a loud crash. Khan had pounced on a nearby curtain tassel, sending the drapes cascading down in a whoosh of fabric.

Jessie laughed. "Trust you to lighten the mood, Khan."

The clever cat blinked innocently up at them. After the day's tense introductions, Khan knew they needed a moment of levity.

Jessie and George shared an amused smile. With Khan's help, they would get to the bottom of this mystery. For now, they had made a solid start, establishing the list of potential suspects. Tomorrow they would begin investigating in earnest, determined to uncover the truth behind the professor's murder and the threats to Lady Evelyn.

Jessie, George, and Khan relaxed in the sanctuary of their makeshift office as the eccentric guests and shifty relatives dispersed throughout Montague Mansion. Jessie saw the door was slightly ajar so pushed it shut. The heavy oak door closed behind them with a thud, leaving the investigators alone with their thoughts.

Jessie perched on the edge of the antique desk, her brow furrowed in concentration. "Well, that was... enlightening," she said finally.

George nodded, leaning back against the wall with his arms crossed. "An intriguing cast of characters, to be sure."

"That's one way to put it," Jessie said wryly. She ticked off on her fingers as she listed them. "The greedy cousins hoping for a cut of the inheritance, the secretive lawyer clearly hiding something, the elusive maid..."

Khan jumped up on the desk, sniffing at Jessie's notes. His tail swished back and forth as he listened intently.

"Yes, they all seem to have potential motives and opportunities," George mused. "But we mustn't judge too quickly. There may be more here than meets the eye."

"Talking of more, the professor's research assistant has made himself scarce," Khan said.

"You know, Khan, that's right. No one has seen him or mentioned him to us. That's rather strange," Jessie said.

"It may be something or it may be nothing," said the enigmatic cat.

Jessie nodded thoughtfully, absently scratching Khan behind the ears. "Too true. I have made a note of that. As for the others, we'll need to observe them more carefully in the coming days. Their actions when they don't think we're watching will be most telling."

"Precisely." George began pacing, his mind whirring through the details. "We must uncover their connections to Lady Evelyn, any past grievances. The tiniest clues could prove vital."

Jessie gazed around the office, taking in the heavy oak furnishings and oil paintings of past Montague lords. She could almost feel the secrets emanating from the walls.

"The answers are here," she said decisively. "Hidden within these rooms, inside the minds of the suspects. We'll find the truth, one way or another."

"I say we search the rooms. The whole mansion from top to bottom," George said.

Khan meowed in agreement. Together, they would unravel this mystery and bring justice for Lady Evelyn. For now, the first seeds had been planted. The investigation was underway.

Seven

THE SEARCH

JESSIE'S HEELS CLICKED AGAINST the hardwood floors as she led George and Khan through the expansive foyer of Montague Mansion. She craned her neck upwards, taking in the vaulted ceilings and crystal chandeliers that glittered overhead.

"Well, this place certainly screams old money," George muttered.

Khan meowed in agreement.

"Let's start with the ground floor and work our way up," Jessie said. "I want to search every nook and cranny. Who knows what secrets this place is hiding?"

They wandered through sitting rooms adorned with antique furnishings and paintings in gilded frames. Jessie trailed her fingers along the spines of leather-bound books in the library, inhaling the earthy scent of aging paper.

Khan leapt onto a reading table, nearly toppling a Tiffany lamp.

"Careful, Khan!" George said. "We don't want to break anything."

The cat flicked his tail dismissively before prowling along the bookshelves. He paused, green eyes narrowing at a section of shelving near the back.

"What is it, boy?" Jessie asked, joining him.

She examined the shelf, noticing faint scuff marks along the wooden base. Gripping the edge, she gave an experimental tug. The entire unit swung outward with a groan, revealing a small hidden room behind it.

"Well done, Khan," Jessie said, scratching the cat behind his ears. She stepped into the dark space, flicking on her torch. "Let's see what secrets this room has been keeping."

Jessie swept her torch beam over the small, dusty room. Cobwebs draped across the corners and a thick layer of dust coated an antique desk and chair in the centre.

"It looks like some kind of hidden study," Jessie mused, moving closer to examine the desk.

George peered over her shoulder as she gingerly lifted the cover of a leather journal sitting atop a stack of papers. The crisp, cream-coloured pages were filled with elegant cursive writing and sketches of hieroglyphics and artefacts.

"This must have belonged to Professor Langford," Jessie said. "Look, these are all notes from his archaeological digs in Egypt."

She slowly turned the pages, pausing when a folded letter slipped out from between the pages. Jessie unfolded it, angling it to catch the beam of her torch.

"It's a letter from someone named Amir Khalid," she said. "He mentions working with Professor Langford in the Valley of the Kings. Listen to this part: 'I appreciate you sending the rubbings of the amulet. I have shown them to my colleagues at the Antiquities Service in Cairo, but none recognise the markings. Perhaps it is tied to the old legends, as you suggest. Please let me know if you are able to unlock its secrets.'"

Jessie met George's gaze, her eyes bright. "This amulet Professor Langford found must have some connection to ancient Egyptian magic. It seems he was obsessed with researching its meaning."

George furrowed his brow. "Well, that gives us a new lead to pursue. We need to find out more about this amulet and why the professor was so fascinated by it."

Khan gave a rumbling meow, as if in agreement. Jessie carefully replaced the letter and journal, her mind spinning with new questions. What were the secrets of this mysterious amulet? And did they hold the key to solving Professor Langford's murder?

Jessie stepped back from the desk, glancing around the hidden room. Her gaze fell on an ornate rug in the centre of the floor. As she studied it, she noticed one corner seemed loose, the fibres frayed.

"Hey, help me move this rug," she said to George.

Together, they pulled the heavy rug aside, revealing a loose floorboard underneath. Ever the boy scout and always being prepared, George grabbed a crowbar from his pack and pried the board up, exposing a dark opening.

"A secret passage!" Jessie exclaimed, shining her torch down into the hole. A narrow stone staircase spiralled into darkness.

George looked at Jessie and grinned. "Shall we?"

Jessie nodded eagerly. "Let's see where it leads."

One by one, they descended the stairs. The temperature dropped noticeably as they went deeper. After several minutes, the stairs opened into a large chamber. Jessie swept her torch around, the beam illuminating stone walls covered in elaborate hieroglyphics and paintings of Egyptian gods and pharaohs. Statues of Anubis, Osiris, and Horus lined the room. In the centre was a large granite sarcophagus.

Khan let out an awed meow. Jessie slowly approached the sarcophagus, running her hand along the cryptic markings engraved on its surface.

"It's like we stumbled into an Egyptian tomb hidden right under the mansion," she murmured. "This must be tied to Professor Langford's archaeological work. But what secrets lie buried down here?"

Jessie carefully circled the chamber, shining her light over the intricate hieroglyphics and statues. She paused as the beam illuminated a small wooden table tucked into an alcove.

"Over here," she called to George.

They approached the table, where an open journal lay next to a flickering oil lamp. Jessie picked up the journal, gently turning the yellowed pages.

"It's another one of Langford's journals," she said. "Look."

She pointed to the name scribbled inside the front cover. As they flipped through, Langford's slanted handwriting detailed his growing obsession with a particular artefact - the Amulet of Atum-Ra. He described it as the key to unlocking ancient Egyptian magical powers.

Jessie's brow furrowed as she read an ominous passage: "He who possesses the Amulet will gain strength beyond imagination but will also be cursed with a terrible fate."

She looked up at George. "If Langford really believed this amulet held some kind of power, it could be the motive for his murder."

"Or the cause of his demise," George mused.

"Possibly," Jessie said.

George nodded grimly. Suddenly, Khan let out a yowl. He was perched atop one of the Anubis statues, pawing at something.

"What did you find, Khan?" Jessie asked as they rushed over.

Wedged into a hidden compartment in the statue was a rolled-up piece of brittle papyrus. Khan looked quite pleased with himself as Jessie carefully removed it. Unrolling the papyrus, they saw rows of cryptic symbols.

"It looks like some kind of map or code," George said. "But what does it lead to?"

Jessie tucked the papyrus into her bag. "Whatever it is, I have a feeling it's the key to unravelling this mystery."

Having second thoughts, Jessie spread the papyrus out on a nearby table, peering intently at the symbols.

"These look like hieroglyphics," she mused. Using one of her reference books in her satchel, she and George slowly translated the ancient text.

"It's directions to a hidden chamber!" Jessie exclaimed. The papyrus map wound through the mansion, marked by secret switches and concealed entrances.

"Let's follow it and see where it leads," George said, excitedly rolling up his sleeves.

With Khan leading the way, they navigated through hidden passageways, locating levers that opened secret doors in the walls. Cobwebs brushed their faces as they descended crumbling staircases into dusty caverns beneath the mansion. Jessie marked their path on a map as they went.

"We must be getting close," she whispered as they reached the end of the papyrus map.

George ran his hands along the wall until he triggered another switch. With a rumble, a section of stones slid away, revealing yet another dark chamber.

Pocket torches in hand, they entered cautiously. The chamber was empty except for a few unlit candles in holders along the walls. Strange symbols and hieroglyphics decorated the room.

"This must be it," George murmured. "But what were we supposed to find here?"

Khan let out an anxious meow. Jessie shivered, feeling suddenly cold. There was a foreboding aura surrounding this hidden place. What secrets lay buried here?

Jessie swept her torch around the chamber, illuminating more dusty artefacts and crumbling scrolls. In the corner stood a large chest, ancient symbols engraved into the wood.

"Look!" she exclaimed. "That chest seems important."

They rushed over and examined the lock. George jiggled the lid but it wouldn't budge.

"We need a key," he muttered.

Jessie thought for a moment. "The skeleton key Lady Evelyn gave to us - that opened all those other locked doors. Let's try it here."

She pulled the ornate key from her bag. With a click it turned in the lock, and the chest creaked open. A puff of dust emerged as they peered inside.

"Scrolls!" Jessie picked one up delicately. The parchment was brittle but the ink still vibrant. "This must be what the map led us to find."

George carefully lifted a scroll. "This one seems to be written in hieroglyphics. Can you read it?"

Jessie scrutinised the symbols. "It describes some kind of ritual with the amulet. There are warnings... something about a curse."

She felt a shiver run down her spine. The scrolls held sinister secrets about the amulet's origins. What had Professor Langford unearthed? Had it led to his death?

Khan made a strange soft rumbling sound as the shadows seemed to shift around them. Jessie rolled up the scroll. "We need to study these further somewhere safer. For now, let's get out of this creepy chamber."

George nodded. "We have a lot of clues to unravel." He packed up the scrolls while Jessie re-locked the chest.

Questions swirled in their minds as they swiftly departed, eager to escape the hidden chamber of secrets.

Jessie and George hurried back through the hidden passageways, scrolls in hand. The shadows seemed to press in around them as they navigated by the beam of Jessie's torch.

"I don't like this place one bit," George muttered. "Let's get out of here fast."

Jessie was about to agree when she heard a noise up ahead. Footsteps, growing louder. She grabbed George's arm and pulled him into a small alcove, switching off the torch. She couldn't see Khan anywhere. They held their breath, hearts pounding.

The footsteps drew nearer, accompanied by a shuffling dragging sound. Jessie peered around the corner and had to stifle a gasp. Professor Langford's hulking figure lumbered by but his features obscured in shadow. He was dragging something heavy.

"It's him!" Jessie whispered. "But how?"

They watched the spectre disappear into the gloom. As soon as it was gone, they scrambled out of hiding and raced back to the mansion's main hallway, nearly colliding with Khan.

"You're back!" the cat exclaimed. "And you brought presents?" He eyed the scrolls.

Jessie scooped him up. "No time to explain. We need to get out of here."

They hurried back to their sanctuary in the makeshift office, minds reeling. The scrolls seemed to confirm the amulet's connection to something sinister. And now Langford's ghost was haunting the mansion. What had they stumbled into? The mystery had taken a dark supernatural twist.

Hearts still thumping from their close encounter, George was the first to speak: "What did we just see back there?" He said, shaking his head in disbelief. "Was that really Professor Langford's ghost?"

"It certainly looked like him," Jessie said. "Though I don't know how that's possible."

Khan chirped up from his perch on the desk. "Perhaps his spirit is bound to the mansion. Many ghosts remain tethered to a location or object associated with their death."

Jessie nodded thoughtfully. "You might be right. It seems the amulet and Langford's research into it may have opened a doorway to the spirit world."

"We need to take a closer look at those scrolls," George said. "There must be more clues about the amulet's power."

Jessie pulled the car over. "Let's review what we know so far." She grabbed a notebook and pen from the desktop.

"The amulet is supposedly connected to an ancient Egyptian curse," she said, jotting down notes. "Langford was obsessed with unlocking its magical powers."

George peered at the scribbled hieroglyphics on the scrolls. "These describe rituals for invoking spirits. So, Langford was meddling with forces beyond his control."

Khan jumped onto Jessie's lap, peering at the notebook. "Yes, he seems to have unleashed dangerous magic. His spirit is likely trapped, unable to rest."

Jessie tapped the pen to her chin. "So' the amulet is key to this mystery. We have to discover its secrets if we're going to solve this."

George nodded. "Langford's ghost must be guarding those secrets. But we're running out of time."

"Then let's keep digging," Jessie said. "There are more clues to uncover. We'll crack this case yet."

"We are still no closer to discovering who sent the letters to Lady Montague," Khan said.

"Perhaps these happenings are all linked," George said.

The trio were determined as they continued their perilous supernatural investigation. The amulet's power was growing, and so was the danger. But they had each other, and mysteries to solve.

Eight

THREATS

Jessie paced back and forth across the ornate Persian rug, her heels sinking into the plush wool with each step. "We need to interview every member of the Montague family time and time again and the staff to get to the bottom of these threats against Lady Evelyn," she said, determination blazing in her hazel eyes.

George nodded, leaning against the marble fireplace mantel. "Hopefully we can uncover the truth about Professor Langford's murder as well."

Khan sat perched on an antique chaise lounge, his tail swishing. "Some of them are bound to let something slip. I'll be watching their every move."

Jessie stopped pacing and gazed around the room. They were gathered in the Montague Mansion's grand drawing room, an ostentatious display of wealth with its gilded furniture, massive crystal chandelier, and floor-to-ceiling oil paintings in gilded frames. It was a stark contrast to the serious nature of their investigation.

"Let's just hope someone here will give us the clues we need," Jessie said. "With a family this eccentric, I'm sure we'll find no shortage of secrets."

Khan's eyes glinted with mischief. "I do love a good family scandal."

George straightened from his perch by the fireplace. "Right. Let's get started then, shall we?"

The game was afoot, and Jessie felt a familiar thrill run through her. The truth was here somewhere, lurking beneath the mansion's opulent surface. She would find it. Failure was not an option.

Jessie turned as the drawing room doors opened and a tall, impeccably dressed man strode in. He had a thin, angular face and piercing grey eyes that swept over them coolly.

"Charles Montague, I presume?" Jessie said.

"Yes." His tone was clipped and dismissive. "Let's get this over with, shall we?"

Jessie studied him closely. Though handsome in a severe way, there was an aloofness to him that immediately put her on edge. She glanced at George and knew he sensed it too.

"Of course," Jessie said smoothly. "We just have a few questions about the threats made against your aunt and her connection to Professor Langford's murder."

Charles' lip curled slightly. "My aunt's affairs are none of your concern."

"On the contrary," George said, an edge in his voice. "We've been hired by Lady Evelyn personally to investigate this matter."

Charles' grey eyes flashed, but he remained silent.

Jessie leaned forward. "Let's start with your relationship with your aunt. Are you close with her?"

Charles let out a derisive laugh. "Hardly. The old bat keeps me on a tight leash. Controls the purse strings, you know."

Jessie raised an eyebrow. "So, you stand to inherit when she passes?"

"Naturally," Charles said coolly. "Though the old girl seems determined to live forever just to spite me."

Khan's eyes narrowed, his tail swishing slowly. Jessie thought she detected a hint of bitterness in Charles' voice.

"And Professor Langford?" Jessie pressed. "We understand he was assisting your aunt with her personal affairs. Did you know him well?"

Charles' expression darkened. "We were acquainted. I didn't care for the man myself."

"Why is that?" George asked.

Charles looked away, a muscle feathering in his jaw. "Let's just say he had a certain... influence over my aunt that I didn't appreciate."

Interesting, Jessie thought. Charles clearly resented Langford's relationship with Lady Evelyn. She made eye contact with George. They were both thinking the same thing. Charles had motive and opportunity if he wanted Langford out of the picture. But did that make him a murderer? Jessie intended to find out. The game was on.

Jessie's thoughts were interrupted by a commotion at the door as a tall, striking woman swept into the room in a flutter of silk and feathers. She paused dramatically in the doorway, one hand placed on her hip, surveying the room with an imperious gaze.

"Dorothy Whitmore makes her entrance," the woman announced in a theatrical voice. She smiled, her crimson lips parting to reveal gleaming white teeth. "No need to stand on ceremony, darlings."

Jessie studied Lady Evelyn's best friend with interest. Dorothy Whitmore was in her late forties, with jet black hair styled in an elegant chignon. Her eyes were lined in kohl, giving her a slightly Bohemian look. She wore an embroidered silk dress in vibrant jewel tones, topped with a feathered shrug. Rings glittered on her fingers as she gestured expansively.

"Mrs Whitmore, thank you for speaking with us today," Jessie began politely. "We appreciate your cooperation with this investigation."

"Anything for my dearest Evelyn," Dorothy declared, swooping down on an armchair. She crossed her legs, regarding Jessie and George imperiously. "I was shocked, utterly devastated by Arthur's murder. What kind of fiend would do something so heinous?"

Jessie nodded sympathetically. "You and Lady Evelyn were close with Professor Langford?"

"Oh yes," Dorothy sighed theatrically. "Arthur was a dear friend. We were like family." Her expression darkened. "Mark my words, someone in this house is behind this. Jealousy, greed - it brings out the worst in people."

Jessie raised an eyebrow. "Do you suspect anyone in particular?"

Dorothy leaned forward conspiratorially. "That nephew Charles has always been power hungry," she whispered. "And the servants - I never trusted any of them..."

"Interesting," Jessie murmured, jotting notes in a small leather journal.

Khan leapt up gracefully onto the arm of Dorothy's chair. The cat fixed his unblinking gaze on the woman, tail twitching.

Dorothy recoiled slightly. "Does he have to sit so close?"

"He's quite harmless, I assure you," Jessie said.

Khan seemed to smirk, eyes glinting knowingly. Jessie had come to rely on the cat's uncanny intuition during investigations. His silent observations often revealed critical clues.

George cleared his throat, redirecting the conversation. "What can you tell us about Professor Langford's relationship with the Montague family?"

Dorothy relaxed, returning her attention to the detectives. "Oh, he and Evelyn were terribly close. Thick as thieves since childhood." She leaned in again, voice lowering. "Rumour was, they were once engaged. But her family didn't approve."

Jessie's eyes widened. This was news to her. "You believe they still had romantic feelings for each other?"

"Without question," Dorothy declared dramatically. "Why else would Arthur leave Evelyn the bulk of his estate?" She sat back with a satisfied smile. "Mark my words, his murder has something to do with that inheritance."

Khan flicked his tail, a subtle signal to Jessie. The cat seemed to sense Dorothy wasn't being entirely forthcoming. Jessie made a mental note to dig deeper into the woman's own potential motives.

"Well, you've given us quite a bit to think about," Jessie said briskly. "We appreciate your help, Mrs Whitmore."

They had gathered valuable insights, but the mystery still lay tantalisingly out of reach.

Jessie stood, signalling the end of the interview. George and Khan followed her lead. As they made their way to the door, Dorothy called after them.

"One more thing, dears."

The trio turned. Dorothy fixed them with an intense look.

"Mark my words. Someone in this house wanted Arthur dead." Her gaze flickered to the door, then back. "And they'll stop at nothing to get Evelyn's money."

A chill went down Jessie's spine. Dorothy's warning echoed her own suspicions. This case was far from closed.

Time for one more question. "Where were you when the professor was murdered?" Jessie said.

Dorothy's gaze turned sharp. "You don't think I had anything to do with this?"

"We have to consider every possibility," Jessie said evenly.

Dorothy huffed. "Well, I never! I was with my bridge club at the time. Ask anyone."

Jessie's instincts hummed. Dorothy clearly adored Lady Montague. But her knowledge of the family's secrets gave her an inside track if she wanted revenge.

Stepping into the hallway, Jessie exchanged a look with George and Khan. "Well, that was certainly enlightening," George murmured.

"And unnerving," Jessie added. "We need to keep digging."

Khan meowed in agreement.

Mulling over the interview, it struck Jessie that Dorothy offered colourful insights into the Montague family dynamics. Charles' coldness toward his aunt. Penelope's money troubles. And the whisper of a codicil to Lady Montague's will that would change everything.

As they walked down the ornate corridor, Jessie's mind raced. The threads of motive were emerging, but the full picture remained obscured. Langford's secret relationship with Lady Montague, the tensions within the family, the lure of inheritance, the amulet... it was a tangled web indeed.

They still had suspects to interview, facts to uncover. But she felt they were on the verge of a breakthrough. The truth was here, lurking in the shadows of Montague Mansion. She just had to bring it into the light.

Jessie led the way to their next interview. The thrill of the hunt quickened her pulse.

Jessie knocked briskly on the door to the sitting room. A muffled voice bid them enter.

Jessie's gaze moved to the young woman perched nervously on the edge of the antique sofa. Penelope Montague was slender and pale, with large doe eyes and trembling hands that fluttered like frightened birds. Jessie guessed her to be in her mid-twenties, but her timid demeanour made her seem much younger.

"Miss Montague, thank you for speaking with us today," Jessie said gently. "We know this must be a difficult time for you as well."

Penelope nodded, twisting a handkerchief between her fingers. "It's just so awful about Professor Langford. And now these threats against Aunt Evelyn..." Her voice quavered.

Jessie exchanged a look with George. The poor girl seemed absolutely terrified.

"We understand you live here with your aunt?" George asked.

"Yes, ever since my parents passed away." Penelope's eyes filled with tears. "Aunt Evelyn has been so kind to take me in. I don't know what I'd do without her."

"And what is your relationship with your aunt? Are you close to her?" Jessie prodded.

Penelope looked down. "I suppose so. Aunt Evelyn has provided for me, but we've never been... confidantes."

"I see," Jessie said. "And you don't have any other family besides your aunt and other cousins?"

Penelope shook her head miserably. "No one. I am an only child. Aunt Evelyn is all I have left... besides my cousins... " She faltered and seemed to fail to finish what was on her mind.

Jessie leaned forward, keeping her tone gentle. "Penelope, are you dependent on your aunt financially?"

The young woman flushed, tears spilling down her cheeks. "I have no money of my own," she admitted brokenly. "If anything happens to Aunt Evelyn, I don't know what will become of me."

Jessie nodded sympathetically. The motive was clear - if Lady Evelyn died, Penelope would be left destitute. But

Jessie sensed the girl's fear was genuine. Someone else may be taking advantage of her vulnerability.

Khan leapt lightly onto the settee, fixing Penelope with an intent stare. She shrank back, clutching her teacup like a shield.

"No need to be afraid," Jessie said gently. "My cat is harmless. He is just curious, like us I suppose, these are merely a few questions about your aunt's situation."

Penelope flinched at the mention of Lady Montague. "Yes, of course. This has all been such a dreadful shock."

"We understand you and your aunt are close."

"Oh yes." Penelope's voice wavered. "Aunt Evelyn has been so generous to me over the years. I don't know what I'd do without her support."

They continued probing delicately, unveiling a portrait of a young woman on the edge of ruin. The more they learned, the more Penelope seemed a likely suspect.

Yet Jessie's intuition prickled a warning. Penelope was fragile, frightened. Was she being manipulated? Or was it all an act?

As the interview ended, Jessie felt they'd uncovered important threads. But Penelope herself remained an enigma - victim, suspect, or both?

Rising to leave, Jessie met George's eyes. A wealth of unspoken communication passed between them. The truth was close now, tantalisingly close. And come what may, they would find it.

They left the interview with fresh leads to pursue. But the case only seemed to grow more complex. Layer upon layer of motive and deception tangled the truth in obscurity.

But Jessie knew with quiet certainty that the answer was here, hidden in this ornate mansion full of secrets. They only had to remain vigilant, and it would reveal itself in time.

Nine

THE RETICENT MAID

BACK IN THE MAKESHIFT office, Jessie and George were reviewing the interviews as Jessie stirred her tea, the silver teaspoon clinking softly against the Spode bone china cup. Across from her, George leaned back in the floral armchair, fingers steepled in thought.

"We'll certainly need to speak with the relatives and each of Lady Evelyn's guests and staff more than once, you know," George said. "There's a motive hidden here somewhere, I'm certain of it."

Jessie nodded. "Yes, we must uncover the truth, though I confess, some of these eccentric characters seem rather intimidating." She smiled wryly. "Fortunate that I have you as a partner in this endeavour."

George returned her smile. "Together, with Khan, we'll get to the bottom of this mystery."

Their conversation was interrupted by raucous laughter from the garden. Jessie peered down from the window to see Charles Montague entertaining the other guests with exaggerated hand gestures, no doubt regaling them with another of his infamous stories.

Nearby stood Lady Evelyn's nephew Edmund, shifting uncomfortably as he tugged at his collar. His eyes darted about furtively, and he flinched when Charles clapped him on the back.

Within hailing distance of the group, hovered the maid, Amelia, her expression guarded as she observed the guests. She kept her hands clasped, shoulders tensed, as though ready to flee at any moment.

Jessie turned back to George. "An odd assortment, though I suspect at least one among them may hold the key to our mysteries." She finished her tea, resolve steeling her nerves. "Shall we begin the hunt?"

George nodded firmly and stood, determination etched on his face. The truth awaited them, and they would uncover it together.

Jessie approached Edmund first, figuring his clear discomfort may make him an easier target.

"Lovely morning, isn't it?" she said brightly.

Edmund jumped, then attempted to arrange his features into a pleasant expression. "Oh, um, yes. Lovely weather."

"The calm before the storm, perhaps," Jessie said lightly. She gestured at the clear blue sky. "Metaphorically speaking, of course."

Edmund tugged at his collar again. "Yes, quite."

"Did you sleep well?" Jessie asked. "I confess, with everything that's happened, rest has been difficult for me."

"Oh, well, you know..." Edmund trailed off, eyes darting away.

Jessie moved closer and lowered her voice. "Between you and me, the motive behind the threats is clear. What do you think?"

Edmund sputtered, face reddening. "I really shouldn't say."

"Come now," Jessie cajoled. "I know you and your aunt have a... complicated relationship. But her situation must be difficult regardless."

Edward looked cornered now, shoulders hunched. "It's true, we have our differences," he admitted. "But I would never wish her harm!" His unnaturally high voice drew curious glances from nearby guests.

Jessie nodded sympathetically. "Of course not. Though with some confusion over her will, I imagine your... financial situation is unstable?"

Edmund grimaced, realisation dawning on his face. "I see. You think I'm after her money." He laughed sharply. "Well, I won't deny being the black sheep, but I'm no blackmailer."

He straightened his jacket, regaining some composure. "Now if you'll excuse me, I should mingle with the other guests."

As he strode off joining the others in the garden, Jessie watched pensively. The seed of suspicion was planted. Now to nurture it carefully and see what bloomed.

George eyed the maid Amelia as she left the garden. Her posture was tense, shoulders hunched and gaze darting about furtively. Interesting. He moved to intercept her path.

"Pardon me, I don't think we've been introduced. George Jenkins, at your service." He gave a shallow bow.

Amelia started, looking flustered. "Oh! I'm just one of the maids, sir, nothing important."

"Nonsense. The staff here are the backbone of this estate. Please, I'd love to learn more about your experience." George smiled disarmingly.

Amelia hesitated, then said, "I'm Amelia, sir. Been working here nigh on ten years now."

"Ten years! You must have seen this household through many changes."

"That I have," Amelia said, warming up slightly. "Her ladyship is a fine mistress to work for. Kind, but fair. Not like some gentry."

"High praise indeed." George's tone grew sombre. "The passing of her friend, the professor, must have been difficult for you."

Amelia's face clouded. "Oh yes. Dreadful shock that was."

"Forgive my impertinence but you seem burdened by something. Is everything alright?" George asked gently.

Panic flitted across Amelia's face. "I... I shouldn't say, sir. Speaking ill of the dead..." She twisted her apron in her hands.

George touched her arm reassuringly. "Please, if you know anything that could help, you must come forward."

Amelia wavered. Finally, voice hushed, she confessed, "Odd things I've seen, late at night. Strangers lurking about the grounds. Whispers behind closed doors. Gave me a dreadful fright."

"How very concerning," George murmured. "Your discretion speaks well of your character. But for Lady Evelyn's sake, we must find the truth."

Amelia nodded reluctantly. "You're right sir. I'll... I'll try to remember more. But please, utter discretion. I need this position."

"You have my word," George vowed solemnly. Amelia nodded and hurried off, casting nervous glances behind her. George's eyes narrowed in thought. There was more here than met the eye.

After his conversation with the reticent maid Amelia, George sought out Jessie to share his findings. He found her in the west wing drawing room, laughing gaily with a woman he recognised as Penelope Montague.

"Ah, George!" Jessie exclaimed. "Of course, you already know Lady Evelyn's niece, Miss Penelope."

"I do," George replied smoothly. "Forgive my intrusion, but might I borrow Jessie for a moment? A matter of some urgency."

"But of course." Miss Penelope's tone was clipped.

Drawing Jessie aside, George recounted his exchange with Amelia in hushed tones. Jessie's eyes widened.

"This proves our suspicions. Something sinister is afoot here."

"Indeed. But we must tread carefully," George cautioned. "The culprit could be anyone."

Jessie nodded. "While you were questioning Amelia, I was getting better acquainted with Miss Penelope. She's a tough nut to crack, very private. But I sensed profound sadness in her."

George raised an eyebrow. "Go on."

"I believe she is quite close to Lady Evelyn. Perhaps if I can gain her trust, she'll confide in me."

"Excellent notion. Your empathy is an asset, my dear." George smiled at her warmly.

Jessie flushed at the compliment. Clearing her throat, she said, "I'll see what I can learn. Let's reconvene later."

With a meaningful glance, they parted ways. Jessie rejoined Miss Penelope, who was waiting expectantly.

"My apologies, Miss Penelope. Mr Jenkins merely wished to discuss arrangements for tomorrow."

"Of course." The woman studied Jessie shrewdly. "You seem an amiable young lady. My aunt speaks fondly of you."

Jessie leaned forward, radiating kindness. "How kind."

Miss Penelope's expression softened almost imperceptibly. "Yes, she values your skills greatly..."

Jessie sensed she was making progress. Gently, she said, "These threats have been difficult for you all. I know you are close to her as well. Perhaps you might find some solace in sharing any confidences that may help to solve these mysteries."

Miss Penelope hesitated, then replied, "I suppose there's no harm in that." She gazed out the window wistfully. "She made such an impression on me as a child. She was always daring, leading us on adventures. How I envied her bravery."

Jessie smiled. "It seems she has never lost that vibrant spirit. But please, go on."

"As I grew older, we drifted apart. Her marriage, my seclusion after my parents died ..." Miss Penelope trailed off, lost in thought.

Sensing there was more, Jessie gambled and prodded delicately. "Though separated by distance, your bond endured. She spoke of you often."

"Did she?" Miss Penelope murmured. She was silent for a moment before continuing. "We reconciled later in life. I shall always cherish that."

Jessie nodded understandingly. She was about to reply when raised voices sounded from the hall. Exchanging a startled glance with Miss Penelope, Jessie hurried to investigate...

Jessie stepped into the hallway, where she saw George in conversation with a middle-aged man dressed in gardening attire - Mr Thompson, the gardener. He was gesturing animatedly, his face flushed, as George listened with a furrowed brow.

Jessie approached discreetly, not wanting to interrupt. She caught snippets of their conversation.

"...acting strange ever since..." the gardener was saying agitatedly.

George nodded. "Go on."

"...swears he saw someone lurking about that night..."

Jessie's eyes widened. This was a promising lead! She moved closer, straining to hear more, when suddenly the gardener glanced over and noticed her and Miss Penelope who had followed Jessie to see what all the fuss was about.

"Here now, what's this?" he blustered, scowling at Jessie. "Another one sticking their nose where it don't belong?"

George stepped in smoothly. "Pay no mind to my colleague. We're simply making inquiries about the night in question." He lowered his voice. "Anything you can tell us would be helpful."

The gardener hesitated, then leaned in and muttered, "I'll not breathe a word of it to anyone but Lady Evelyn herself." With that, he turned on his heel and marched off.

Jessie exchanged a look with George. "Well, that was rather cryptic," she remarked.

"Indeed. He seems to have pertinent information but is reluctant to share it." George furrowed his brow. "How do we gain his trust?"

Jessie pondered this. Then her face lit up. "I think I know just the person who can help with that." She hurried off down the corridor, George following curiously...

Ten

THE COOK

JESSIE MARCHED TO THE kitchens with George following her as quickly as he could. They found Mrs Patterson bustling about preparing dinner.

"Good evening, Mrs Patterson," Jessie said brightly. "I wonder if I might have a word?"

The cook eyed them suspiciously. "What's this about then?"

"It's about Mr Thompson, the gardener," Jessie said. "We understand he's been acting rather odd lately. We were hoping you could provide some insight into his behaviour."

Mrs Patterson folded her arms across her ample chest. "And why should I tell you anything about him?"

George stepped forward, giving the cook his most charming smile. "We only want to get to the bottom of things, same as you. Any information at all could be critical."

Mrs Patterson wavered, then gestured for them to come closer. In a low voice, she said, "He's been jittery ever since the professor died. Jumping at shadows and the like. I asked him what was wrong once, and he said..." She dropped her voice even lower. "He said he saw something that night. Something unnatural."

Jessie and George exchanged a glance. "How intriguing," Jessie murmured. "Did he say what it was?"

But Mrs Patterson shook her head. "That's all I know. But I reckon whatever he saw has him spooked good and proper."

"Thank you, you've been most helpful," George said warmly, while Jessie nodded in agreement. Excusing themselves, they left the kitchens with a spring in their steps.

"This confirms the gardener knows something important about the night of the murder," Jessie said. "Now we just need to get him to tell us what it is."

George nodded thoughtfully. "I have an idea how we might manage that..."

Jessie and George made their way outside to the gardens, keeping an eye out for Mr Thompson. The grounds were quiet in the fading evening light, with no sign of the gardener.

"He's probably tucked away in one of the sheds," George murmured. "We should split up to cover more ground."

Jessie nodded. "I'll check the potting shed by the roses. You try the tool shed near the maze."

They split up, each creeping quietly through the manicured hedges and flower beds. Jessie approached the little potting shed, its windows dark. As she reached for the handle, she heard voices inside - a man and a woman, locked in a heated argument. Jessie froze, listening intently.

"...you have to tell them what you saw!" the woman whispered fiercely. "This has gone on long enough."

"I can't, it's too dangerous," came the man's anxious reply. Jessie recognised the voice - it was Mr Thompson! "You don't understand what I'm dealing with."

"The police can protect you," the woman insisted. "This is about justice!"

Jessie's pulse quickened. They had to be discussing the professor's murder! She leaned closer, holding her breath to catch every word. This could be the lead they needed to crack the case wide open!

Eleven

THE SCENE OF THE CRIME

HAVING DECIDED TO LOOK again at the scene of the crime, Jessie, George, and Khan entered Professor Langford's cluttered room, their eyes scanning the haphazard collection of artefacts and books that lined the shelves. Jessie wrinkled her nose at the musty odour that permeated the space.

"Well, this is quite the mess," George murmured, gingerly stepping over a pile of dusty tomes.

Khan's tail swished back and forth as he prowled along the floorboards, his whiskers twitching. "I'm sensing something hidden amongst all this clutter," he remarked, pausing by an old mahogany desk.

Jessie moved to join him, her hazel eyes bright with interest. As she examined the desk, Khan suddenly leapt up onto it, nearly knocking over a precariously stacked pile of papers.

"Hey, watch it!" George cautioned as he rushed to steady the teetering documents.

Khan ignored him, pawing intently at a section of carved wood panelling along the back of the desk. His claws caught on a nearly invisible groove.

"Aha, a secret compartment!" Jessie exclaimed. She carefully worked the panel free, revealing a small hollow space inside. Her breath caught as she withdrew a leather-bound journal from within.

"This must be Langford's personal diary," she murmured. "It could contain all kinds of clues about his obsession with the amulet."

Khan sat back on his haunches, looking smug. "All in a day's work for a magical cat," he purred.

George rolled his eyes but couldn't hide his own eagerness as they gathered around the journal. "Let's see what secrets this old book is hiding," he said. Their search for answers had led them here, and now they were one step closer to unravelling the mystery.

Jessie reverently opened the journal, the old pages crackling softly as she turned them. The first entry was dated over a decade ago, the slanted handwriting detailing Professor Langford's acquisition of the amulet at an auction in London.

"He says here it's Babylonian in origin," Jessie murmured, scanning the text quickly. "He believed it was imbued with magical properties from the start."

She flipped ahead, pausing on an entry from a few years later. "Listen to this - 'The amulet glows faintly in moonlight. When I wear it, I feel strength and vitality beyond my years. It is a conduit to forces unseen!'"

Jessie looked up, meeting George's gaze. "It seems Langford truly believed in the supernatural powers of the amulet."

George frowned thoughtfully. "Did it really possess magic, or was the professor delusional?"

Khan twitched his tail. "Perhaps a bit of both," he mused. "An object like that likely held power, but it may have warped Langford's mind over time."

"We need to learn all we can about it," Jessie said, returning her attention to the journal. Each new entry revealed more of Langford's growing obsession, his experiments with the amulet, and his conviction it could unlock mystical secrets.

What had started as scholarly curiosity had transformed into a dangerous fixation. Jessie could feel the professor's fervour leaping from the page. She shuddered, hoping they could discover the amulet's origins and purpose before it claimed any other victims.

Jessie closed the journal slowly, looking up at George and Khan with concern in her eyes.

"This changes things," she said. "We can't dismiss the amulet as merely an archaeological curiosity anymore. If Langford's writings are true, it possesses real power - power we don't fully understand."

George nodded, his brow furrowed. "Agreed. We need to learn all we can about its history and supposed magical properties. There may be a connection between the amulet and Langford's murder that we're missing."

"Perhaps it is cursed, and that is why it was stolen from him," Khan suggested, his tail swishing back and forth.

Jessie chewed her lip thoughtfully. "Cursed or not, Langford's obsession with unlocking its secrets seems to have taken over his life. His writings make it clear the amulet had become more important to him than anything else."

She paused, meeting George's eyes. "Do you think ...could the amulet have somehow driven him to his death?"

George looked uneasy at the thought. "I don't know. But I think we can't exclude any hypothesis. We are dealing with the unknown."

Khan nodded solemnly. "There are dark forces at work here. To get to the truth, we must trace the amulet's path through history and legend. Its secrets may be dangerous, but we must uncover them."

Jessie tucked the journal securely into her bag. "Then let's get started. We have a mystery to solve."

Jessie, George, and Khan left Professor Langford's cluttered office, the professor's mysterious journal secured safely in Jessie's bag. As they walked down the hallway, Khan's tail swished back and forth nervously.

"I sense an ominous energy surrounding that amulet," the cat remarked. "Its origins may lie in ancient Egyptian magic - powerful forces we cannot begin to understand."

Jessie nodded, her hazel eyes troubled. "If what Langford wrote about its supernatural properties is true, it could be very dangerous. We need to learn all we can about it."

"Where should we start?" George asked. "Libraries? Museums? There must be some reference to it somewhere if it's as old as Langford believed."

Khan's eyes gleamed knowingly. "My cat senses tell me the university archives may be a good place to begin. But tread carefully, my friends. If the amulet is cursed, our investigation could awaken things better left undisturbed."

Jessie smiled wryly at the mystical cat. "Don't worry, we'll be careful. But one way or another, we're going to get to the bottom of this mystery."

The three continued on their way, determined to uncover the secrets of the amulet and its connection to Professor Langford's untimely death. The answers they sought might unlock powerful magic...or unleash dangerous forces beyond their control.

Jessie's mind raced as they walked, piecing together the clues so far. The threats to Lady Evelyn, the amulet, the professor's obsession, his mysterious death - it couldn't all be coincidence. This case had taken a dark turn, and she sensed they were on the verge of a dangerous discovery.

Glancing at George, she could tell her friend shared her unease. But the determined glint in his eye mirrored her own. They would find the truth, no matter the cost.

Khan padded along silently beside them, his wise gaze missing nothing. She was thankful for the mystical cat's help, though his warnings about ancient curses made her nervous. But she knew his skills would prove invaluable in the challenges ahead.

"The archives first," Jessie declared as they exited the building. "We'll pore over every scrap of information we can find about the amulet. Its origins, its history, any legends attached to it over the centuries."

George nodded. "If it has supernatural powers, there must be some record of them. We'll dig until we uncover the amulet's secrets."

Jessie squared her shoulders, ready for the battles to come. Now she knew the professor's death was no accident. Dark magic was at work, and she would stop at nothing to bring his killer to justice.

With her friends at her side, she would solve this mystery. No curse would deter her from revealing the truth hidden behind the amulet's gleaming facade. The hunt was on.

Jessie glanced down at the ancient journal in her hands. Its worn leather binding and faded pages contained knowledge that had led to the professor's demise. She was determined to uncover its secrets without falling prey to the same forces.

"We need to study this carefully," she said. "Every notation, every scribbled margin - it could hold clues about the amulet's power."

George nodded, his expression grim. "And we must take precautions. Strange forces are at work here." He gestured to Khan, the mystical cat pacing alongside them. "Our friend's warnings make that clear."

Khan's green eyes glinted with wisdom. "Dark magic leaves traces. I will know if we stray too close."

Jessie felt emboldened having the mystical feline as an ally. With his help, surely they could solve this mystery without succumbing to the sinister powers surrounding the amulet.

As they stepped out into the sunshine, Jessie squared her shoulders. "No curse will stop us from finding the truth."

George met her determined gaze. "We will unravel the secrets held within these pages." He held up the journal.

"And bring a killer to justice," Jessie added fiercely.

Together, the three unlikely investigators strode purposefully away from the office. The hunt was on.

Jessie nodded. "We'll unravel this mystery together."

As they stepped outside, she squared her shoulders in determination. The hunt was on to expose the secrets contained within the journal's pages. To solve a murder, bring a killer to justice, and face the supernatural forces emerging from the shadows.

Jessie met George's eyes with a fierce resolve. Then they strode forward into the unknown, with Khan leading the way. The adventure was just beginning.

Jessie took a deep breath as they entered the library, inhaling the familiar scent of aged paper and leather bindings. She always felt at home among the towering shelves, each packed with stories and information waiting to be discovered.

Today, however, they had a specific purpose - researching the history and meaning behind the engraved amulet found with Professor Langford's body.

Khan leapt up onto a table, peering intently at the ancient journal they had found concealed in the professor's office. "This tome is our first clue," he remarked, green eyes flashing. "But more obscure knowledge is needed to unravel the amulet's origins."

Jessie nodded, rolling up her sleeves with determination. "Let's get to work. Khan, you check for any references to Egyptian artefacts or occult texts. George, gather books on symbols and runic languages. I'll dig into the archives for folklore about enchanted objects."

George gave her shoulder a supportive squeeze. "We'll figure this out together," he said firmly.

Jessie felt herself smiling despite the dark mystery enshrouding them. With her intellect, George's logic, and Khan's supernatural instincts, they made a formidable team.

Shelves groaned as they pulled down book after book, searching for connections. Sunlight faded and lamps flickered on as hours passed in studious silence.

Until finally Khan's ears perked up from his spot on a pile of manuscripts. "Listen to this," he murmured, jade eyes gleaming...

The hunt for answers had begun in earnest. And with each new clue, they drew closer to unveiling the secrets of the amulet and solving Professor Langford's murder.

Twelve

Mr Baxter's Office

JESSIE PACED THE LENGTH of the lavish study used by Mr Baxter as his office at the mansion. She paused to run her fingers over the spines of leather-bound books that lined the shelves, their gilded titles glinting in the afternoon sun.

"He should have been here by now," she said, turning to George who stood stiffly by the grand mahogany desk.

George checked his pocket watch for the third time. "It's not like Baxter to be late. Do you think he caught wind of the reason behind our meeting?"

Jessie sighed, her nerves fraying. They had arranged this rendezvous with Baxter to confront him about the amulet found near the dead body. According to Evelyn, Baxter had been researching similar occult artefacts just before the murder. Surely, he must know something.

But with each minute that ticked by, Jessie's confidence wavered. Had they made a mistake in suspecting Baxter? Her intuition, normally so clear, felt clouded.

She caught a glimpse of herself reflected in the dark windowpane. The fiery sunset illuminated her auburn hair like a halo. If only she had a real angel on her shoulder, instead of just George. She stifled a nervous laugh.

"I suppose all we can do is wait," George said. He gave her shoulder a gentle squeeze, as if sensing her uncertainty. She managed a small smile. Waiting had never been her strong suit.

Jessie continued pacing She again paused to examine a framed photograph on the mantle showing a young Evelyn with her late husband. Evelyn hardly spoke of him but judging by the adoring look in her eyes in the photo, they must have been deeply in love.

Jessie wondered if she'd ever find a love like that. A little voice that sounded suspiciously like Khan whispered, "Perhaps closer than you think, my dear." She shook her head, ignoring the preposterous thought.

At that moment, the study door flew open and Mr Baxter strode in, face flushed. "My apologies for being late," he huffed.

His eyes narrowed when he saw Jessie and George. "To what do I owe the pleasure?" Though his tone implied anything but pleasure.

"Thank you for joining us, Mr Baxter," George said evenly. "We hoped you could assist in a... delicate matter."

Baxter's jaw tightened. "Go on."

"I believe you've been researching certain occult artefacts as of late," Jessie began carefully. "Items like a certain jewelled amulet?"

Baxter tensed. "My research is my own business. Now if you've nothing else-"

"Oh, I think you know why we're interested in that amulet," Jessie pressed, her gaze fixed on him. "The one found by the body."

Baxter paled slightly but quickly recovered. "I have no idea what you mean. Now if you'll excuse me... "

He moved to leave but George blocked his path.

"Not so fast," George said. "We know you've been meeting with Lady Evelyn about this artefact. Withholding information would be unwise."

Baxter scowled. "I'll not stand here and be interrogated by amateurs. Now let me pass!"

Jessie stepped closer, eyes blazing. The truth was within reach, she could feel it. All she needed was for Baxter to slip up.

"Just tell us what you know about the amulet," she implored. "Please. Lives depend on it."

Baxter faltered, seeming to wrestle with indecision. Finally, he sighed, shoulders slumping in resignation. "Very well. I'll tell you everything I know."

Baxter moved to the desk and rifled through a stack of papers. He retrieved a leather journal and flipped it open.

"This is where I've recorded my research on various occult artefacts," he explained. "Including the amulet you mentioned."

He slid the journal across to Jessie and George. Jessie's eyes rapidly scanned the pages, looking for mentions of the jewelled amulet.

"Here," Baxter said, pointing to a detailed sketch and description. "I've been tracking the amulet's whereabouts for some time. It last surfaced at an estate auction three months ago and was purchased by a private collector."

Baxter met their gazes. "On the night of the... incident, I was hosting a gathering at the Liverpool Law Society. Nearly a dozen guests can verify I was in attendance the entire evening."

Jessie's heart sank. She exchanged a disappointed look with George. Their prime suspect had an ironclad alibi.

"Blast," George muttered under his breath, then louder, "We were certain you were involved somehow."

Baxter shook his head. "My interest was purely academic. But I swear to you both, I've no connection to this crime."

Jessie sighed, frustration mounting. Their one solid lead had just unravelled before their eyes.

Where did they go from here? Doubts crept in as she questioned her detective skills. Perhaps this case was too much for her after all. Perhaps Baxter was right, she was an amateur.

Despite Mr Baxter's solid alibi, it was clear he was still holding something back. His answers were too neat and rehearsed.

Jessie fixed him with an intense stare. "You may not have committed the murder yourself, but I suspect you know more than you're letting on."

Baxter bristled at the accusation. "Now see here, I've cooperated fully-"

"Have you?" George interjected sharply. "Withholding evidence is hardly what I'd call cooperative."

Baxter's face reddened. "How dare you! I'll not stand here and be insulted after proving my innocence."

Jessie crossed her arms. "Then tell us about your relationship with the victim. It's obvious you two had a history."

"That's neither here nor there," Baxter sputtered.

"We'll be the judges of that," George said. "Either you talk, or we go to the authorities with our suspicions."

Trapped, Baxter sank into a chair with a huff. Jessie and George exchanged a knowing look. The tension in the room was palpable as they closed in on their cagey suspect.

Jessie's mind raced as they grilled Baxter. Though he had an alibi, his behaviour was highly suspicious. She had to get to the truth, but her confidence was shaken.

What if she'd hit another dead end? Doubt crept in as she questioned her sleuthing skills. This case seemed to grow more complex by the day. Would her amateur detective work be enough?

And then there was George. Try as she might, Jessie couldn't ignore her growing feelings for him. She cherished their partnership but longed for something more. Could such a distraction prove dangerous with a killer on the loose?

Shaking herself, Jessie refocused on Baxter. They still had a murder to solve, personal matters aside. She'd sort out her heart later.

Back at their makeshift office, Jessie slumped into a chair with a sigh.

"Cheer up, old girl," Khan said, sauntering over. "We'll crack this case yet."

Despite everything, Jessie smiled. The cat's swagger and wit never failed to lift her spirits.

"Yes, we will," she said, scratching Khan behind the ears. "Baxter is clearly hiding something. We just have to keep digging."

Khan purred, leaning into her hand. "That's the spirit. And you know George and I will be by your side every step of the way."

At the mention of George, Jessie felt her cheeks grow warm.

"Oh ho, what's this?" Khan said with a knowing smirk. "Got a touch of the love flu, have we?"

Jessie swatted him playfully. "Oh, hush, you."

But she couldn't help glancing over at George and feeling that now familiar flutter in her heart. With loyal friends by her side, she could get through anything - even the scary thrill of falling in love.

Jessie took a deep breath to steady her nerves. There was no time for daydreaming - not when a killer was on the loose.

"Right, let's review the facts," she said, grabbing a notepad. "Baxter claims he was in Liverpool when Professor Langford was murdered. We need to verify his alibi."

George nodded. "Bill Roberts can do that in jiffy. I'll call him."

"Good idea," Jessie said. "In the meantime, I'll search Baxter's study again. There may be something there he doesn't want us to find."

Khan stretched lazily. "While you two run your errands, I'll cosy up to the maids. They're a chatty bunch - maybe they know something. All I need do is listen in whilst they feed me scraps. I must say the scraps here are delicious... caviar every day."

Jessie smiled. "Excellent. We'll reconvene this evening and share anything we uncover."

The three exchanged determined glances, ready to pick up the trail. The mystery was deepening, but with grit and teamwork, they would unravel it yet.

Jessie felt a swell of gratitude for her partners in crime-solving. With Khan's charm and George's steadfast loyalty, she could conquer any challenge. And if their search yielded new clues, they'd be one step closer to nabbing the culprit.

Leaving George to call Bill Roberts, and once Khan had left in search of scraps, both delicacies and information,

Jessie made her way to Baxter's study which served as his office in the mansion.

The thrill of the hunt quickened her pulse, but a pang of anxiety remained. Something in Baxter's manner still seemed off. She only hoped their hunch proved right - and that no more innocent lives would be lost before they brought this mystery to its satisfying close.

She approached the heavy oaken door of Baxter's private study once more, hoping her search this time would yield the evidence needed to crack the case wide open.

Inserting the skeleton key, Jessie stepped inside. The study was dim, lit only by the silver glow of the full moon streaming through the towering, mullioned windows. Shadows danced across the walls between the hulking bookshelves and antique furnishings.

Moving carefully so as not to disturb anything, Jessie began her search. She examined the surface of Baxter's massive mahogany desk first, rifling through the stacks of papers and ledgers. Nothing but mundane legal correspondence and accounting records.

Next, she moved to the bookshelves, scanning the titles and gently removing select volumes to check if anything was hidden within. Most were innocuous legal texts on torts and contracts, and a smattering of classics of literature. No clues there.

As Jessie made her way around the room, she paused to admire an original, exquisite Tiffany lamp on a side table. Its stained-glass shade cast kaleidoscopic patterns across the wall. Lady Evelyn certainly had impeccable taste.

Finally, Jessie arrived at the large globe against the back wall. She remembered Baxter fidgeting with it earlier when confronted. Grasping it gently, she rotated the globe and examined the base. Aha! A small latch was visible under one edge. Heart racing, Jessie popped it open to reveal a hidden compartment containing a small leather-bound journal.

This had to be what Baxter was hiding. Hands trembling, Jessie opened the journal. What secrets did it contain?

Jessie flipped through the journal, skimming page after page of Baxter's tight script. Most of it was mundane - appointments, research notes, gardening schedules. Nothing about the amulet or the murder. She was just about to close it in disappointment when an entry towards the back caught her eye.

It was dated a few weeks before the murder. Baxter wrote about acquiring a rare artefact from a private collector, an ancient amulet with strange markings and an ominous aura. He didn't fully understand its purpose but could sense its dark power.

Jessie's pulse quickened. This had to be the amulet they were searching for! She read on eagerly. Baxter experimented with the amulet, wearing it during meditations and feeling its energy course through him. But it also disturbed him, filled his mind with violent thoughts and vivid nightmares.

The final entry described locking the amulet away, unable to bear its malevolent presence any longer. But where had he hidden it? Frustrated, Jessie flipped the page only to find the remaining sheets ripped out.

Footsteps in the hall jolted her from her thoughts. Quickly, she pocketed the journal and clicked the globe compartment shut. She had found a critical clue, but the mystery was far from solved. More determined than ever, Jessie slipped from the study into the shadows, journal in hand. The hunt continued.

Thirteen

Charles Montague

Jessie tapped her foot impatiently as she waited for George to finish his cup of tea. Khan was perched on the study windowsill, tail flicking back and forth.

"I'm telling you, Charles is up to something," Jessie said. "My intuition is telling me he's up to no good."

George set his teacup down with a clatter. "I agree, but we've no proof. We need hard evidence if we're to confront him."

"Then let's search his room," Jessie said. "If he's in league with this Mr Baxter, there must be some trail."

George hesitated. "Snooping around a guest's private quarters seems rather uncouth."

Khan chimed in with a meow of agreement. Jessie shot him a look.

"Desperate times call for desperate measures. Besides, we are private investigators and that's what we are supposed to do and on top of that, we have carte blanche from Lady Evelyn to do what it takes short of killing someone." She stood. "I'll keep watch while you search. We must uncover the truth."

George sighed but followed Jessie out of the room. They crept upstairs to the east wing where Charles was staying. Jessie kept her eyes peeled for any sign of movement while George tried the door. Finding it unlocked, he slipped inside.

Jessie paced the hallway, nerves jangling. She hoped they weren't on a wild goose chase. But her intuition told her Charles was tangled up in this mess somehow.

George emerged a few minutes later, face grim. "You were right. Take a look." He opened a book to reveal a hollowed-out interior containing letters. Jessie's eyes widened as she scanned the incriminating contents, including payments to an unknown associate.

"I knew it!" Jessie said. "Now we have leverage to get the truth out of him."

George nodded, a deep furrow in his brow. "This confirms he is not who we thought. What a disappointment."

"Who you thought, George. Just because he was an officer in the Great War doesn't automatically make him a gentleman."

Khan swished his tail, eyes narrowed. The game was afoot.

Jessie and George made their way downstairs, evidence in hand. They found Charles in the study, seemingly relaxed as he perused a book. He glanced up as they entered, surprise flickering across his face.

"Miss Jessie, Mister George, what can I do for you?"

Jessie crossed her arms. "You can start by explaining this." She held up the hollowed-out book.

Charles paled. "Where did you get that?"

"Your room," George said grimly. "Care to explain the hidden letters? The payments?"

Charles stood abruptly. "You had no right to go rifling through my private belongings!"

"We had every right when a guest and relative turns out to be a suspect in death threats sent to Lady Evelyn and the professor's murder," Jessie shot back.

Charles faltered. "Murder? What are you talking about?"

Jessie stepped closer. "The game is up. We know you're connected to Mr Baxter and were involved in this whole sordid scheme."

Charles shook his head frantically. "No, you don't understand. I had my reasons, but I never wanted anyone hurt."

George slammed his hand on the desk. "Your reasons? Lady Evelyn took you in like her own son and this is how you repay her trust? With betrayal?"

Charles turned ashen. He sank into a chair, head in hands. "You're right, of course. I've made a mess of everything. But please, let me explain..."

He went on to lay out his motivations in detail - his gambling debts, Mr Baxter's threats, the payments he received for information about Lady Evelyn's wealth. With each revelation, Jessie and George's expressions hardened. The depth of his duplicity was staggering.

Finally, Charles finished, anguish etched on his face. "I know it's unforgivable. I'll accept whatever consequences come. But believe me, I never intended for it to go this far."

Jessie shook her head in disgust. "Your intentions don't matter now. Only the truth does." She turned on her heel, George following. The damage was done. Now they had the professor's murder to solve.

Jessie and George stepped out into the hallway, closing the door firmly behind them. Lady Evelyn stood there, worry creasing her brow.

"What's happened?" she asked. "I heard raised voices."

Jessie hesitated. There was no gentle way to break this news. "I'm afraid we've uncovered some...troubling things about Charles. He's been less than honest with you."

Lady Evelyn paled. "What do you mean?"

"He's been communicating secretly with Mr Baxter," George said gruffly. "Providing information about your affairs. We believe he was involved in a plot against you to manipulate your will and go against your wishes..."

"No." Lady Evelyn swayed slightly, grasping the wall. "Not Charles. He would never..."

Jessie guided her to a chair, crouching beside her. "I'm so sorry. We didn't want to believe it either. But the evidence is clear."

Tears filled Lady Evelyn's eyes. "After everything I've done for him...I took him in when he had nothing. Treated him like my own son." She buried her face in her hands. "My dear boy... how could he?"

Jessie squeezed her shoulder gently. In the study, they could hear the faint sounds of Charles weeping. The quiet heartbreak of betrayal hung over the mansion like a pall.

After a moment, Lady Evelyn lifted her head. Her expression was stony. "I want to speak with him. Alone."

"Of course." Jessie helped her stand.

Lady Evelyn squared her shoulders and marched to the study door. She paused, hand on the knob. "Thank you for telling me the truth," she said softly. "I know it wasn't easy."

Then she entered the room, closing the door behind her with an air of grim finality. Jessie and George exchanged a look. The damage was done, the secrets laid bare. Now Lady Evelyn would handle the rest in her own way.

Jessie, George, and Khan retreated to the library to discuss their next steps.

"Well, that's torn it," George said, collapsing into an armchair. "Never thought Charles would be involved in something like this."

Khan leapt up onto the desk, tail swishing. "I could smell his guilt from the start. But betraying one's own family..." He shook his head. "Deplorable."

Jessie leaned against the desk, arms folded. "I feel responsible. We should have realised sooner."

George waved a hand. "Don't blame yourself. Charles had us all fooled." His expression darkened. "But why? Money?"

"He did seem obsessed with inheriting the estate," Jessie mused. She sighed, running a hand through her auburn hair. "I suppose this derails our investigation. We're back to square one without Charles' information."

Khan's eyes gleamed knowingly. "Perhaps not. Charles may yet prove useful."

Jessie and George looked at him in surprise.

"Useful?" George said. "He lied to us, conspired against his own aunt—"

"Desperation drives people to folly," Khan interrupted, lashing his tail. "Charles is weak, not evil. I suspect he can still be...persuaded...to cooperate."

Jessie caught Khan's meaning. "You think we can convince him to keep feeding us information? Even after we exposed him?"

Khan purred. "Everyone has a price. We need only determine his."

The study doors burst open and Charles stumbled in, face streaked with tears. He froze at the sight of them.

Jessie straightened. "Well, speak of the devil..."

Jessie fixed Charles with a steely gaze, arms folded across her chest.

"I suppose you're here to gloat," Charles spat bitterly, wiping his eyes with the back of his hand.

"Hardly." Jessie's voice was icy. "We're here for the truth."

Charles let out a hollow laugh. "Haven't I told you everything already?"

Jessie stepped towards him. "You've told us plenty of lies. Now it's time for the full truth, no more games."

Charles staggered back. "Please, Jessie, I never meant for it to go this far..."

"But it did," she retorted. "And now a man is dead because of your greed."

Charles paled. "You can't pin Langford's death on me! All I did was pass information to Baxter, I never meant—"

"You betrayed our trust!" Jessie shouted, her composure finally cracking. "You betrayed your family, your aunt, all of us!"

Charles cringed at her words.

Jessie took a breath, steadying herself. "It's time to take responsibility. No more lies, no more omissions. Tell us everything and face the consequences."

Charles' shoulders slumped in defeat. When he finally spoke, his voice was a broken whisper.

"Where do you want me to start?"

Jessie crossed her arms. "From the beginning. And leave nothing out this time."

Charles nodded slowly, pulling a chair over to sit down. Jessie and George exchanged a look, then settled in to listen. The truth was finally emerging from Charles' lips.

George paced the room, his fists clenched at his sides. "I should never have trusted you," he seethed, glaring at Charles. "To think, I thought of you as a reliable source in this investigation."

Charles hung his head. "George, please, let me explain—"

"Explain what?" George snapped. "How you sold confidential information to further your own greedy ends? How you betrayed your own flesh and blood for a few quid?"

Charles flinched at the accusation. "It wasn't as simple as that," he pleaded. "I was desperate, I needed the money—"

"And that justifies destroying lives?" George roared.

Jessie placed a gentle hand on George's arm. "Getting angry won't change what's been done," she said softly.

George trembled with rage but held his tongue.

Charles looked between them helplessly. "I never meant for it to spiral like this," he croaked. "Truly, I didn't think anyone would be harmed."

Jessie fixed him with a piercing stare. "But someone was harmed, Charles. Your aunt's friend is dead because of the chain of events you put into motion."

The colour drained from Charles' face. "My God, you're right," he whispered. "This is all my fault." He dropped his head into his hands.

Jessie pulled up a chair across from Charles. "You still have a chance to make this right," she said, her voice firm but not unkind. "Tell us everything you know. No more secrets. No more prevarication."

Charles lifted his head, shame and regret etched on his features. "Where do I even begin?" he asked softly.

"Start at the beginning," Jessie replied. "We're listening."

Charles took a deep breath and started unravelling the truth, as George and Jessie leaned in intently. The damage was done, but perhaps Charles could still redeem himself by helping them find justice for Lady Evelyn.

Charles spoke haltingly at first, still clearly ashamed of his actions. But as he continued, the words began to pour out faster, the whole sordid tale emerging. How he had conspired with Baxter to siphon away some of Aunt Evelyn's fortune. How they had planned to arrange her marriage to the wealthy but reclusive Gabriel Lockwood, to gain access to the Lockwood estate as well. And most importantly how Baxter had paid some ruffian to write the death threats to Lady Evelyn.

"It was a long con," Charles admitted. "But once Aunt Evelyn hired you ... the plan fell apart. Baxter turned on me. He demanded more money to keep quiet about my involvement."

"Blackmail," George growled.

Charles nodded. "I've made a right mess of everything. I don't know how I'll ever make amends."

Jessie studied him intently. "Helping us bring Baxter to justice would be a start."

"Of course, anything you need. Just tell me what to do," Charles said eagerly.

Jessie glanced at George, who still looked wary but gave her a small nod. Turning back to Charles, she said, "We'll be in touch. For now, just lay low."

Charles nodded, relief washing over his pale face.

After Charles had departed, Jessie let out a long breath. "Well, that was..."

"Unexpected," George supplied.

"And difficult," Jessie added. She reached down to scratch Khan behind the ears. The cat purred contentedly, reminding her that despite the emotional upheaval, life carried on.

"What now?" George asked. "Can we even trust anything he said?"

Jessie considered for a moment. "I think he was being truthful. Whether he can make up for the damage, I don't know. But we have another lead to follow."

George nodded slowly. "Baxter."

"Right. And we won't stop until we unmask him for the swindler he is and bring the professor's killer to justice," Jessie said resolutely.

George gave her a small smile. "Right, we won't and the two episodes may be connected. "

Together, they gathered their things, hearts heavy but hope still glimmering. The mystery was far from over.

Jessie stared out the window of the study, watching the rain patter against the glass. The dark clouds seemed to match the sombre mood that had settled upon Montague Mansion since the professor's murder.

Fourteen

DARK MAGIC

IN THE MAKESHIFT OFFICE, Jessie and George reviewed the latest revelations. Khan agreed that their collective intuition was probably correct: there was something not quite right about Charles Montague's so-called confessions.

Deciding the mansion held more secrets that could shed light on the professor's murder, the trio set off to explore once more. Jessie trailed her fingers along the dusty wall as she, George, and Khan crept down the dark hallway. Cobwebs clung to the corners and shadows danced across the peeling wallpaper, but something about this passage called to her.

"We're getting close," she murmured. "I can feel it."

George nodded, one hand resting on Jessie's shoulder. Khan's eyes glowed green in the darkness. With a flick of his tail, the cat darted ahead, stopping before an ornate mirror hanging askew.

Jessie's breath caught. She reached out, heart pounding, and slid the mirror aside to reveal a small, hidden door.

"Well done, Khan," she whispered. The cat preened.

With bated breath, Jessie eased the door open. Beyond lay a tiny room coated in years of undisturbed dust. Her sharp eyes landed on a delicate scroll tucked into a niche in the far wall.

"The scroll," George gasped.

Jessie crossed the room reverently and lifted the ancient papyrus. Intricate hieroglyphics marched across its cracked surface. What secrets did it hold? She longed to unravel its mysteries, but danger lurked in these symbols.

Khan peered at the scroll, eyes flashing. "Dark magic resides here," he rumbled. "We must take care."

Jessie nodded, hands trembling. "Then let's shed some light on this curse before it's too late."

Jessie gently unrolled a section of the ancient papyrus, holding her breath as the brittle scroll threatened to crack and crumble in her hands. The intricate hieroglyphics were faded with age, but she could make out depictions of ominous creatures and rituals.

"Can you read it?" George asked, peering over Jessie's shoulder.

Khan's eyes glowed as he studied the symbols. "It speaks of a dark pharaoh who sought eternal life through a profane ritual," the cat murmured. "His hubris brought a terrible curse upon himself and his kingdom."

Jessie's skin prickled with unease. She scanned the scroll, picking out references to blood sacrifices, unholy pacts, and vengeful gods. This was dangerous knowledge that had been buried for centuries.

"We have to stop this curse before the amulet unleashes its power again," she said.

George squeezed her shoulder reassuringly. "We'll figure this out together. But we should get the scroll somewhere safe before-"

A cold blast of air suddenly whipped through the hidden room, magically snuffing out their torch beams. Jessie gasped as the papyrus was ripped from her hands.

Khan's eyes flashed in the darkness. "The spirits sense our meddling," he warned. "We must go, now!"

Heart pounding, Jessie groped blindly for George. This curse ran deeper than she could have imagined. What had they stirred up?

Jessie's heart pounded as she groped in the darkness for George. The scroll had been ripped from her hands by an unseen force, and a bone-chilling breeze swirled through the hidden room.

"We need light," she said, trying to keep her voice steady.

"Allow me," Khan rumbled. The cat's eyes glowed brighter, casting an eerie illumination over the dusty chamber. Jessie quickly scanned the room but saw no sign of the ancient papyrus.

George put a reassuring hand on her shoulder. "We'll find it again. But Khan's right, we should leave this place."

Jessie nodded, a shiver running down her spine. There was a palpable sense of menace in the air now. She couldn't shake the feeling they were being watched by some vengeful spirit.

Khan led the way out of the hidden room, his lantern-like eyes piercing the gloom. Jessie and George followed close behind, groping along the cold stone walls.

"What do you think happened to the scroll?" Jessie whispered.

"Taken by those who wish to keep its secrets buried," Khan replied ominously, "the same people or thing that killed the university archivist before the sergeant could speak to him."

They hurried through the maze of dust-choked corridors and back into the main halls of the mansion. But the sense of lurking danger did not abate.

Jessie knew they had stirred up perilous forces. She feared where this investigation might lead them next. But the fighter in her was determined to break the curse and solve this mystery.

Jessie, George, and Khan regrouped in the mansion's grand library. Despite the warm glow of the fireplace, a chill lingered in the air.

"That scroll must hold the key," Jessie said, breaking the uneasy silence. "It's connected to the amulet, I'm sure of it."

George nodded. "Those hieroglyphics mentioned some kind of ritual. A way to activate the amulet's powers."

"Powers we do not fully understand," Khan added solemnly. His intense green eyes reflected the firelight. "There are forces at work here beyond the realm of the living."

Jessie suppressed a shudder at the grave tone in Khan's voice. Ever since they discovered that secret chamber, an ominous cloud had descended upon their investigation.

"We have to keep searching," she said firmly. "Maybe the answers are here in the library."

But as she scanned the endless rows of leather-bound books, doubt crept into her mind. What had they gotten themselves into? Were these ancient secrets meant to remain buried?

George gently touched her hand. "We're in this together," he said softly.

Jessie managed a small smile. At least she didn't have to face this alone. With George and Khan by her side, she felt brave enough to carry on.

Come what may, they would see this mystery through to the end.

Jessie carefully examined a large textbook titled 'Pharaohs and Magic.' There in the middle of the book was a photograph of the ancient papyrus scroll that had been snatched from her. A closer look revealed the same intricate hieroglyphics covering its yellowed surface.

She scanned the symbols, brow furrowed in concentration as she tried to decipher their meaning. "This mentions some kind of invocation," she murmured. "A ritual to summon an ancient spirit."

Khan's ears twitched, his eyes narrowing. "The scroll speaks of darkness and fire," he rumbled. "Of a vengeful god demanding sacrifice."

George paled, glancing between Jessie and the scroll apprehensively. "Sacrifice? This is getting stranger by the minute."

"There's more," Jessie said. "Something about the amulet being a conduit, a way to channel the spirit's power." She traced a line of hieroglyphs with her finger. "But the price is steep. The ritual requires a blood offering."

"Blood?" George swallowed hard. "You don't think it means..."

Jessie met his worried gaze. "Human sacrifice. That's what it's implying." A cold finger of fear stroked her spine.

Just what had they stumbled into? This was no ordinary Egyptian curse. The scroll spoke of darkness beyond imagination, of an ancient evil that should never be awakened.

Khan's fur bristled, eyes flashing in the firelight. "We tread a dangerous path," he warned. "But turning back now may prove even more perilous."

Jessie closed the book with trembling fingers. She had to be strong, to see this through. But the ominous secrets they'd unearthed left her shaken to her core.

Jessie took a deep breath, trying to steady her nerves. This investigation had taken a dangerous, potentially deadly turn. She glanced at George and Khan, seeing her own tension and fear reflected in their faces.

"We need to figure out our next move," she said, voice low but firm. "Before whoever cursed this amulet tries to stop us."

Khan nodded solemnly. "Agreed. We cannot let these dark forces deter us from the truth."

George ran a hand through his hair, exhaling shakily. "Right. But where do we go from here? The scroll mentioned a ritual, but..."

"We find a way to break it," Jessie said. "To lift the curse, without unleashing something even worse." She placed the book securely back on to the shelf. "There must be more clues, more pieces to this puzzle. We just have to put them together."

"And quickly," Khan added. "I sense a sinister presence lurking in these very walls. Watching. Waiting."

A chill swept through Jessie. The cat was right - she felt it too. An oppressive weight, a gathering gloom just out of sight. They were running out of time.

"Then let's keep looking," she said. "There's an answer here in this mansion somewhere, I know it."

George managed a shaky smile. "Right beside you, partner. No matter what we find."

Jessie returned a grateful smile, then headed for the door. Khan slunk after her, fur on end, ears swivelling. The hunt continued.

They had stumbled onto something ancient and malevolent. But she could not turn back now. No matter the cost, Jessie had to see this through.

Lives depended on it.

Fifteen

The Vengeful Spirit

THE FLICKERING GLOW OF the gas mantles cast eerie shadows across the walls of the study. Jessie sat hunched over the antique desk, brow furrowed in concentration as she pored over the weathered pages of Professor Langford's journal.

"The amulet is the key," she murmured. "With it, the wielder can summon and control spirits."

George paced back and forth across the Turkish rug, hands clasped behind his back. "Yes, but to what end? Why would someone unleash a vengeful spirit in Lady Montague's home?"

Jessie traced her fingers over the faded hieroglyphics sketched in the journal's margins. "Someone who wants access to the treasure hidden on the estate, possibly. A vengeful spirit wouldn't need reason to force Baxter into arranging to send the threats to lady Evelyn. But how to stop them?"

A soft thud drew her attention. Khan leapt up onto the desk, tail swishing as he batted playfully at a precariously stacked pile of books. Jessie rescued them just before they toppled over.

"All right, no more distractions." She lifted the black cat onto her lap, where he purred contentedly. "We need to find a way to break this curse."

With Khan curled up beside her, Jessie reached for a heavy tome on ancient Egyptian magic. There had to be something within these pages that could help banish the vengeful spirit. She was determined to protect Lady Evelyn and solve this mystery, no matter what the cost.

Jessie flipped through the dusty pages, scanning for any mention of curses or rituals. Khan's steady purring was a soothing backdrop as she searched.

"This is getting us nowhere," George said, breaking the silence. He paced over and put a hand on the book, forcing Jessie to stop turning pages. "We can't just sit here reading. We need to take action."

Jessie frowned, gently moving his hand aside. "Getting ourselves killed won't help anyone. We need more information first."

"Information won't stop a vengeful spirit." George's jaw was set stubbornly. "We have to find the amulet and destroy it."

"Destroying the amulet could make things worse." Jessie kept her voice calm, trying not to rise to the bait of George's brashness.

He threw up his hands in frustration. "So, we do nothing? Wait for this spirit to harm Lady Evelyn?"

Jessie slammed the book shut, making Khan's ears flick in surprise. "I'm not suggesting we do nothing. But we can't rush in without a plan. That never ends well for anyone."

She met George's eyes steadily across the desk. Khan looked between them, as if gauging the sudden tension in the room.

Finally, George sighed and ran a hand through his hair. "You're right. I just feel so powerless, and I hate it."

Jessie reached over to squeeze his hand. "I know. But we'll figure this out, together."

Khan bumped his head against their joined hands and purred louder, as if in agreement. Despite the dangers they faced, they weren't without hope. Jessie had to believe that.

Jessie took a deep breath to steady her nerves. She knew Lady Evelyn was counting on her to solve this mystery and stop the vengeful spirit before anyone else got hurt.

Research was Jessie's forte, a skill acquired as a former librarian. She dived back into the ancient texts on Egyptian magic, determined to uncover the key to breaking the curse. There had to be some ritual or counter-spell that could help them. She wasn't about to let some centuries-old spirit threaten her friends.

Khan jumped up on the desk, nosing at the open books. He let out a questioning "Meow?" and looked up at Jessie with his intelligent green eyes.

"You're right, this curse on the amulet seems not only linked to the murder of the professor and the archivist but also connected to the threats against Lady Montague," Jessie said, scratching the cat behind his ears. "If we can break the curse, we might just stop the spirit's power."

Khan purred his agreement and went back to peering curiously at the arcane symbols on the weathered pages. Meanwhile, George searched through the library stacks, trusting in his instinct to uncover whatever obscure text or magic ritual they needed.

Jessie smiled to herself. Together, they would crack this case. She had absolute faith in her and George's combined skills. And with Khan's clever intuition on their side, no vengeful spirit stood a chance.

Jessie glanced up from the ancient text she was studying as George emerged from the depths of the library, clutching a leather-bound manuscript.

"I think I've found something," he said, brushing dust off the cover.

Khan's ears perked up and he trotted over to inspect George's find, giving it an inquisitive sniff.

"It appears to contain details about an ancient Egyptian ritual used to break curses and banish vengeful spirits," George explained. "Just what we need."

"Excellent work, George," Jessie said. "Let's take a look."

As they pored over the arcane instructions, Khan let out a dubious "Mrrp?"

Jessie smiled and scratched under the cat's chin. "I know, it seems a bit far-fetched. But at this point, I think we have to try anything that might stop this spirit."

George carefully copied down the ritual's ingredients and steps. Jessie gathered the rare herbs and artefacts required - wormwood, acacia, crushed lapis lazuli. The musty library took on an aura of mystery and anticipation as she prepared the ceremonial tools.

Khan watched all this solemnly, still evidently sceptical about their chances. But he stayed close, offering his steady companionship.

Jessie took a deep breath, focusing her mind. She had to believe in herself and her skills. Too much was at stake now to fail. With George and Khan by her side, she would break this curse and send the vengeful spirit back where it belonged.

Jessie took a deep breath as she reviewed the ritual instructions one last time. This was it - the moment to confront the vengeful spirit and break its sinister hold over Montague Mansion.

She wished she felt more confident. Doubt crept in, making her hands unsteady as she arranged the artefacts and herbs. What if she botched this ritual? What if her knowledge wasn't enough? Lady Evelyn and the others were depending on her. Failure could put them all at risk.

Khan seemed to sense her hesitation. He bumped his head against her hand gently, then went over to circle around George's legs, meowing insistently.

"You're right, Khan," George said. "We can do this. We've unravelled tricky situations before, haven't we Jessie? Like the time we broke that warlock's enchantment. Or when we cleansed Sir Percy Hardwicke's estate of that mischievous poltergeist."

Jessie smiled, memories of their past adventures restoring her resolve. George was right - together, they had overcome far stranger mysteries than this. The spirit may be powerful, but it was no match for her research, George's level head, and Khan's watchful eye.

"You're absolutely right," she told George, straightening up. "We've got this. That spirit has plagued this house long enough. It's time for it to move on."

George grinned and gave her shoulder an encouraging squeeze. "That's the spirit. Let's go end this curse once and for all!"

Khan chirped his assent and shook his fur out eagerly, ready to back them up. With her friends' faith shoring her up, Jessie led the way out of the library. The final confrontation awaited.

Jessie took a deep breath as she slowly opened the door to the east wing drawing room. This was the room Lady Evelyn had described feeling an ominous presence in, seeing flickering shadows from the corner of her eye.

As the door creaked open, a musty chill emanated from within. Jessie felt the fine hairs on her neck stand up. George and Khan crowded close behind her as she stepped inside, their shapes barely visible in the gloomy chamber.

Heavy velvet drapes blocked out all natural light. Strange symbols and circles had been etched into the hardwood floor, remnants of Professor Langford's occult experiments. The outlines of the arcane markings seemed to writhe and shift as Jessie's eyes struggled to adjust.

She could feel it now - the malicious energy permeating the space, like a lurking, hateful gaze tracking their every move. The vengeful spirit was here, and it knew they had come to banish it from this world.

Jessie set her bag down and began removing the ritual components they had gathered earlier. George helped lay them out carefully in a circle while Khan prowled the room's perimeter, alert for any spectral attacks.

Jessie lit the candles and incense, their flickering glow providing small islands of light in the oppressive darkness. The musty herbs filled the air with their cleansing smoke as Jessie began the incantation. The words of banishment felt heavy on her tongue.

The temperature dropped sharply, the candles guttering. Jessie's breath misted before her as an unnatural wind swirled through the confined space. The spirit was resisting, but she pressed on with the ritual.

There was a crackling energy in the air now, raising the hairs on her arms. The circle of artefacts began to rattle violently against the floor. Jessie had to raise her voice to be heard over the mounting spectral din.

"George, the sage!" she yelled. He tossed her the bundle and she waved the pungent smoke in a circle, reinforcing their spiritual defences. She continued the incantation, nearing the ritual's climax. The spirit's rage grew, but Jessie would not be deterred. With one final verse, a pulse of light burst from the circle of artefacts.

The room fell eerily still and calm once more. Jessie held her breath, scarcely daring to hope they had succeeded. But the oppressive presence was gone. The vengeful spirit's reign of this house was finally over.

Jessie let out a long exhale, the tension in her body releasing. They had done it. The vengeful spirit was banished.

Khan sauntered over and wound between her legs, purring loudly. "Nice work, Jessie. I knew you had it in you," he meowed.

George stepped forward and pulled Jessie into a tight hug. "That was incredible! I've never seen anything like it." He smiled at her proudly.

Jessie returned his smile, exhilarated by their success. "We make a pretty good team, the three of us."

Khan hopped up on the table, nosing at the artefacts. "So, what happens now? Do we just leave these lying around for the next ghost to use?"

Jessie laughed. "Good point. We should find somewhere safe to store them."

As they discussed what to do with the ritual objects, Jessie felt a deep sense of satisfaction. Together they had overcome an ancient evil using courage, quick thinking, and trust in one another. She knew that no matter what lay ahead, with George and Khan by her side, she could face any challenge. The paranormal was their forte.

Sixteen

Murky Clues

Jessie stared into the depths of her coffee, as if the bitter liquid could provide answers to the endless questions swirling through her mind. This case was proving far more complex than she had anticipated. Doubt gnawed at the edges of her confidence, threatening to unravel the tenuous threads of progress she had made.

With a heavy sigh, she set down the cup and ran both hands through her auburn hair. The weight of responsibility pressed down on her shoulders, the fate of the investigation resting squarely on her intuition. But the clues remained murky, the way forward unclear. Yes, the spirit was clearly behind much but had any humans played a part apart from Baxter and Charles' conspiracy?

She began pacing the length of the office, frustration brewing with every step. What if she failed? The thought sent a chill down her spine. This case could make or break her reputation, not to mention her business partnership with George.

Jessie paused by the window, arms wrapped around herself as if to keep from coming apart. The view outside provided no solace, only a reminder of the ticking clock. Time was running out and she still had nothing solid to go on. So far, only curses, vengeful spirits and rituals.

Turning sharply, she strode to the corkboard covered in scrawled notes and crime scene photos. It was a chaotic web of disjointed facts and vague theories. Useless. Crumpling a page in her fist, she fought the urge to sweep it all aside in a dramatic show of pique.

Instead, she leaned forward, palms flat on the board, and took a deep, steadying breath. The sound of the ringing study telephone jarred her from the temporary calm. Jessie hesitated only a moment before deciding to ignore the caller. She couldn't bear to hear the inevitable questions from anyone. Not when doubt still plagued her so. She needed clarity first, that spark of revelation that would restart her stalled investigation and rekindle her belief in her abilities. Until then, she would tackle this solo. Chin up and eyes narrowed in determination, Jessie turned back to the board. She had a mystery to solve.

Jessie stared at the board, willing the disjointed clues to coalesce into a coherent picture. But the longer she looked, the more muddled it all became. Doubt crept in once more, insidious tendrils threatening to choke out her confidence.

She squeezed her eyes shut, pressing the heels of her hands against them until bursts of light exploded across the darkness. A small mewl made her drop her hands and open her eyes.

Khan sat watching her, his tail swishing lazily. "Rough day at the office, detective?" the cat asked, a wry note in his voice.

Jessie huffed out a humourless laugh. "That's one way to put it. I feel like I'm grasping at straws here, Khan."

She gestured helplessly at the board. "All these bits and pieces that I can't seem to fit together no matter how hard I try."

Khan tilted his head, regarding her thoughtfully. "Sometimes you just need to step back and clear your head. Come sit. Take a cat nap." He patted the space beside him.

Jessie sighed but sank down cross-legged on the floor. Khan immediately climbed into her lap, kneading her legs as he circled and settled. His rumbling purr vibrated through her as Jessie slowly stroked his fur. The simple act soothed her fraying nerves.

"Don't be so hard on yourself," Khan said gently. "You've cracked far more challenging cases than this one."

Jessie shook her head. "Have I though? Maybe I've just been lucky so far. And that luck is finally running out."

Khan swatted her arm with his paw. "Hey now, enough of that defeatist attitude. You're Jessie Harper, supernatural detective extraordinaire. A little obstacle isn't going to stop you."

Despite herself, Jessie smiled slightly. "You always know how to deliver a pep talk, don't you?"

The cat arched his back proudly. "It's a gift. Now chin up, detective. You're the best."

Jessie took a deep breath and nodded, feeling the weight on her shoulders lighten. "You're right. I can do this. I just need to approach it from a new angle."

Khan purred approvingly. "That's the spirit. The game's afoot, Watson!"

Jessie stroked Khan's fur as she mulled over the case details again in her mind. There had to be something she was missing, some clue that would break this mystery wide open.

Her gaze drifted across the room and landed on George, who was poring over a stack of old newspapers, searching for leads. Jessie studied his profile - the furrow in his brow, the focused look in his warm brown eyes. Over the past few weeks working together, she'd come to appreciate his quick intellect and dry sense of humour. Not to mention he was easy on the eyes...

Jessie shook her head slightly. Now was not the time for those kinds of thoughts. They had a professional partnership; anything more would only complicate things. Still, when he glanced up and caught her eye, giving her a small smile, Jessie felt a little flutter in her chest before quickly looking away.

Khan, perceptive as always, noticed the exchange. A devious look entered his eyes. "You know what you two need? A break to clear your heads. And I know just the thing!" He leapt up and bounded over to the bookshelf, knocking several volumes to the floor.

George jumped at the sudden commotion. "What the devil..."

"Whoopsie daisy!" Khan exclaimed. "Jessie, be a dear and help George pick those up."

Jessie shot Khan a look, knowing exactly what he was up to with his orchestrated "accident." But she got up and joined George on the floor, reaching for the fallen books.

Their hands brushed as they both grabbed for the same book. Jessie felt her cheeks grow warm. "Sorry," she mumbled.

"It's alright," George said. Was he blushing too? Jessie sneaked a glance at him as they tidied the rest of the books. Their eyes met and they both laughed nervously.

Khan sat back, tail swishing with satisfaction over his handiwork. Perhaps those two just needed a little push in the right direction.

Jessie stood up, holding the stack of books in her arms. "Well, that was..."

"A bit clumsy," George supplied, smiling as he too got to his feet.

Jessie chuckled. "Yes, clumsy is one word for it."

They replaced the fallen books in silence. Jessie was acutely aware of George's presence beside her, his arm brushing against hers as he slid a book onto the shelf. Her heart skipped a beat.

Once the books were back in order, they regarded each other awkwardly. The moment stretched between them.

Finally, Jessie cleared her throat. "So... shall we get back to the investigation then?"

George nodded, though he seemed reluctant to return to business. "Of course. What were we looking into next?"

Jessie hesitated. An internal debate waged within her - should she open up about her doubts, or keep them bottled up? She wavered, then decided to take a leap.

"George, can I confess something?" she began nervously. "I've been feeling...unsure. About my abilities, I mean. To solve this case." She looked down, unable to meet his eyes. "What if I'm not cut out for this after all?"

George was quiet for a moment. Then he placed a hand on her shoulder. "Jessie, look at me." She raised her eyes. His gaze was earnest. "You are one of the most talented investigators I know. Your skills and intuition are unmatched. If anyone can crack this case, it's you."

Jessie felt a lump form in her throat. "You really believe that?"

"Absolutely," George said firmly. "I've seen you achieve the impossible time and again. A little self-doubt is normal. But don't let it consume you." He gave her shoulder a supportive squeeze. "I have faith in you, Jessie."

Jessie managed a small, grateful smile, blinking back tears. "Thank you, George. I needed to hear that."

He smiled back. "Anytime. That's what partners are for, right?"

Jessie nodded, feeling lighter than she had in days. With George by her side, she could face this case with renewed determination.

Jessie took a deep breath, regaining her composure. The supportive exchange with George had lifted her spirits. She was ready to dive back into the investigation refreshed and raring to go.

"Alright, where were we?" she said, surveying the cluttered desk covered in case files and notes.

"I believe we were cross-referencing the guest lists from the night of the murder," George replied, shuffling through some papers. "Trying to spot any anomalies between the various eye-witness accounts."

Jessie nodded. As they returned to the task at hand, the mood lightened. George told a silly anecdote about a mishap at a recent event he'd attended, and Jessie found herself laughing.

"Honestly, these high society functions are just one disaster after another," George chuckled.

"Tell me about it," Jessie said, grinning. "I have enough stories to fill a book."

Their banter continued as they worked. Jessie realised how much she enjoyed George's company. He had a quick wit and charming manner that perfectly complimented her own. She felt at ease around him, able to be fully herself.

The search for a breakthrough in the case was temporarily forgotten as they swapped entertaining tales from past adventures. Jessie couldn't remember the last time she'd smiled and laughed this much during an investigation.

Leave it to George to help her find moments of lightness and joy, even amidst the gravity of this mystery. She was struck by how perfectly their energies aligned. More than just colleagues, they made quite the team.

Jessie leaned back in her chair, sighing contentedly. The laughter and easy rapport with George had lifted her spirits. "Well, I think that's enough reminiscing for now," she said. "We should refocus our efforts."

George nodded in agreement. "You're right. But I'm glad we took a moment to unwind."

He smiled warmly at Jessie, and she felt a flutter in her chest. She quickly looked down, pretending to shuffle through some papers.

"Yes, it was a nice break," she said softly.

They returned to analysing the case notes, sitting in comfortable silence. After some time, Jessie stumbled upon a connection.

"Aha, look here," she said, scooting her chair closer to George's. "These three guests all sat at table seven during dinner."

She leaned in, pointing to the names on the list. Her shoulder lightly brushed George's arm. He turned towards her, their faces inches apart. Jessie met his gaze, noticing the striking dark brown of his eyes.

"Well spotted," George said quietly. "This could be a promising lead." But he made no move to pull away.

Jessie's heart quickened. The air between them seemed to crackle with electricity. Slowly, tentatively, George reached out and tucked a loose strand of hair behind Jessie's ear. She shivered at his touch.

Neither spoke. The moment hung suspended, both unsure what came next. But there was no denying the connection blossoming between them. The kiss could wait...for now, it was enough to share this perfect intimate moment.

Seventeen

ANOTHER MURDER VICTIM

JESSIE SANK INTO THE worn leather armchair, glancing around the library's oak shelves and rows of dusty books. George leaned against the fireplace mantle, arms folded, while Khan perched on the back of the sofa, tail swishing.

"Well, we're in quite the pickle this time," Jessie sighed, rubbing her temples. "Charles Montague murdered, another mysterious locked room. We have to solve this fast before the killer strikes again."

George nodded grimly. "No doubt this is connected to Professor Langford's case. The locked door, the lack of forced entry or exit, the baffling lack of evidence."

"Yes, the similarities are too precise to be coincidental," Jessie agreed. "It seems we have a serial killer with a penchant for the impossible on our hands."

Khan's ears twitched. "The question is, what motivated our murderer to target these particular victims? Revenge? Jealousy? Greed? Or something more... sinister?" His green eyes narrowed in thought.

Jessie tapped her chin. "Langford was on the verge of a major archaeological discovery according to his journal. Perhaps he discovered something valuable?"

"Hmm, a solid lead to pursue," mused George. "We'll need to speak to his colleagues and the professor in Egypt and dig deeper into his work. I'll take that angle. I am sure Lady Evelyn will permit a long-distance telephone call."

Jessie nodded. "And I'll investigate Charles' background for connections. There must be a link we're missing." She shook her head in frustration. "But we must act quickly, before the killer can disappear or strike again."

George clenched his jaw. "Agreed. We don't have any time to waste."

Khan licked his paw casually. "Well then, let's get cracking, shall we? I do love a good mystery."

Jessie nodded, a determined glint in her hazel eyes. "Right. We all know what we have to do."

She turned and led George and Khan out of the library, down the dark hallway towards Charles Montague's bedroom. The local constabulary had cordoned off the crime scene and the heavy oak door stood ajar. Steeling herself, Jessie stepped inside.

The metallic scent of blood hung thick in the air. Jessie's gaze swept over the scene, taking in every detail. The victim lay sprawled on his back across the four-poster bed, limbs akimbo. His throat had been cut, blood soaking into the brocade bedspread beneath him.

"Hmm... not quite like Langford," George murmured, crossing his arms with a grave expression.

"Just as dead, it seems," Khan said.

Jessie nodded slowly, moving closer to examine the body. The victim's face was frozen in an expression of utter terror, eyes and mouth wide. His hands were clenched into white-knuckled fists, fingernails digging into his palms. Whoever had done this, he had seen them coming.

Khan leapt lightly onto the bed, sniffing delicately near the gaping wound. "Hmmm..." His tail twitched thoughtfully. "No signs of a struggle. It seems our killer appeared and disappeared as if by magic, just as before."

Jessie chewed her lip. There had to be an explanation. She refused to believe it was actual magic at work. Her keen investigative mind sorted through theories, searching for the hidden thread that would unravel this impossible crime.

The game was afoot, and she would not rest until justice was served.

Jessie carefully examined the victim's hands, prying open the stiff fingers to reveal deep crescent-shaped cuts in the palms.

"He clenched his fists so tightly that he broke the skin," she murmured. "He must have seen the killer approach just before..."

Her voice trailed off as she noticed something clutched in the victim's right hand. Gently, she worked it free.

It was a scrap of paper, edges rough where it had been hastily torn from something larger. Scrawled across it in shaky handwriting was a single word: "Revenge."

Jessie's eyes widened. She held up the paper for George to see.

"This is new evidence," she said. "It seems the killer left some kind of message."

George took the paper, frowning. "Revenge for what?"

Khan leapt down from the bed, tail held high. "Excellent find, Jessie! The plot thickens most satisfactorily."

He padded over to examine the note himself, sniffing it delicately. "Hmm...the paper smells of pipe tobacco. Perhaps our victim had a smoking companion shortly before his demise?"

Jessie tucked the scrap carefully into an evidence bag. "We need to figure out what this revenge note means. It's our first real clue."

Her mind whirred with possibilities. The game was on, and the thrill of the hunt quickened her pulse. She was certain that with persistence, she would uncover the truth behind these confounding crimes.

Justice would be served. She would make sure of it.

Jessie's excitement over the new evidence was tempered by a creeping sense of unease. Time was not on their side - if they didn't act quickly, the killer could claim a third victim, possibly Lady Evelyn herself.

She exchanged a tense look with George. "We need to move faster," she said urgently. "Who knows when or where they'll strike again?"

George nodded, his expression grim. "Agreed. We should split up to cover more ground. I'll start reviewing our list of potential suspects and see if I can discover a motive."

"And I'll dig deeper into the similarities between the two murders," Jessie said. "There must be a connection we're missing."

Khan gazed up at them, eyes glinting. "Capital idea. I shall lend my deductive prowess to whichever avenue of inquiry needs it most." He paused, ears twitching. "Do be careful, both of you. Our adversary is cunning and ruthless."

Jessie felt a shiver run down her spine at the warning. This was no ordinary killer they faced. She steeled herself, refusing to let fear deter her from finding the truth.

"We'll get to the bottom of this," she vowed. "No one else will suffer the same fate. Not if I can help it."

With that, she hurried off to the study used as their makeshift office to pore over the case files, mind racing. The clock was ticking - lives hung in the balance. Failure was not an option.

Jessie settled into the study's cosy reading nook, files and notes spread out on the table before her. She was searching for any links between the two victims - Professor Langford and the more recent murder of Charles Montague. Both were killed in locked rooms under seemingly impossible circumstances. There had to be something she was missing.

As she cross-referenced dates, locations, backgrounds, a nagging thought tugged at her. Langford's research assistant, Oscar, had been acting strangely ever since the murder - jumpy, evasive. Was it just grief and shock? Or something more? The young man had opportunity and access that others lacked.

Jessie tapped her pen on the table. Oscar may be a promising lead, but he could also be a distraction, a red herring keeping her from the real killer. She hated to think ill of him without cause yet had to consider every possibility.

Just then, Khan sauntered over, tail swishing casually. "No luck finding connections yet, I see," he remarked, leaping up beside her notes. His eyes narrowed, fixed on one name. "This Oscar fellow... he may merit closer inspection, despite appearances."

Jessie nodded slowly. "I was just thinking the same. What's your thoughts?"

Khan tilted his head, gaze unblinking. "There is more to him than meets the eye. But tread carefully - dangerous waters lie beneath the placid surface."

Jessie shivered but felt resolved. Oscar may prove innocent, but she couldn't afford to dismiss any promising lead. Not with lives at stake. She gathered up the files with fresh determination. The truth was out there, waiting to be uncovered.

Jessie took a deep breath and knocked firmly on Oscar's guest room door. When it swung open, the young man's eyes widened in surprise.

"Jessie! What are you doing here?" His voice sounded high-pitched, nervous.

She offered a sympathetic smile. "So sorry to bother you, Oscar. I just had a few follow-up questions about Professor Langford's research. May I come in?"

Oscar hesitated, shifting his weight between feet. "Uh, now's not really a good time..."

Jessie pressed on gently. "It will only take a moment." She paused, meeting his anxious gaze. "I know how difficult this must be, with the tragedy so fresh. But it's important we get to the truth of what happened."

Oscar's shoulders slumped in resignation. "Alright, fine. Come on in."

Jessie stepped inside the modest room. Her eyes darted around keenly, searching for any telling details amidst the cluttered mess.

She sat on the worn sofa and withdrew her notepad. "Let's start with the night of Langford's murder. Can you walk me through your whereabouts that evening?"

Oscar perched tentatively across from her. "I already told the police everything."

"I know but humour me. Sometimes revisiting events jogs new memories." Jessie kept her tone light, despite the gravity of her mission. Lives depended on what Oscar knew.

The young man fidgeted with his shirt hem, avoiding her gaze. "Well, I left the village pub around eight in the evening. You can check that with Mrs Willoughby. She is on the garden festival committee. Then I stopped to buy some fish and chips and walked back here eating them on the way. Spent the rest of the evening going through case files for Professor Langford's next lecture."

Jessie nodded encouragingly. "And you didn't notice anything unusual? No one following you, nothing out of the ordinary? Did you notice anything unusual as you walked through the mansion grounds?"

Oscar shook his head, but something in his manner seemed off. Evasive.

Jessie's instincts prickled with suspicion. She leaned forward intently. "Are you sure, Oscar? This is critical. You can trust me."

He blinked rapidly, face draining of colour. "I... I don't know anything!" His voice rang with desperation. "Please, you have to believe me!"

A heavy silence fell between them. Jessie weighed her options. Oscar was clearly afraid, holding something back. But pushing too hard might spook him into total silence. She needed his trust.

Softening her tone, she said gently, "It's okay, Oscar. Take a deep breath." She handed him a glass of water from the table. He gulped it down, hands trembling.

"I know you're scared. But working together, we can get to the bottom of this. I promise, whatever you tell me stays between us." She held his frightened gaze, willing him to confide in her. Lives hung in the balance.

Eighteen

A Hoax

Oscar finally divulged what he knew about the dark power of the amulet but made it clear he was only repeating what the professor had told him. George and Jessie also asked him what he knew about the Ghost Orchid to see if it had any connection to the murders.

"It's a hoax," Oscar assured them and went on to explaining the hoax started at the nearby West Lancashire annual garden festival when bored flower enthusiasts from all over the country gathered to celebrate the region's vibrant blooms, but this year, they fabricated a story about the mysterious Ghost Orchid, a rare and elusive flower said to be native to the depths of the South American rainforest.

Oscar continued to tell how he noticed the growing obsession with the Ghost Orchid among the festival visitors of which he was one. The mysterious flower had become the talk of the festival, overshadowing the real mystery at hand—the professor's murder.

He had spoken with one of the festival committee members and was told in confidence that the whole thing about the orchid having magical properties was utter nonsense. Oscar added, "However, he urged me to keep that quiet as a friend of Lady Evelyn had bought the specimen and seemed to believe in its magical properties. Little did he know that friend was Professor Langford."

"That was Mrs Willoughby then who divulged these confidences to you?" Jessie said.

"Yes, so she not he," Oscar said sheepishly.

Jessie and George were engrossed in Oscar's story and believed him. They could not help but marvel at the deceptive allure of the Ghost Orchid—a red herring that had briefly captured the area's imagination, only to be overshadowed by the shadowy secrets and hidden motives that lay within the confines of Montague Mansion.

That orchid also now lay within the mansion's conservatory. Now they knew it was harmless and had no connection to the murders nor the threatening letters, Jessie and George decided there was no point in enlightening Lady Evelyn.

Satisfied Oscar could offer no further assistance, Jessie, George, and Khan decided on the next steps in this complex investigation.

The full moon cast an eerie glow over the expansive grounds of Montague Mansion as Jessie, George, and Khan approached the west wing under the cover of darkness. Jessie clutched an ancient Egyptian scroll, while George carried a bag of sacred artefacts - protection against the evil they knew lurked within.

Khan's fur stood on end, his senses heightened. "I don't like this, not one bit," the mystical black cat muttered. "But it must be done."

Jessie nodded, her eyes glinting with determination in the moonlight. "We stick to the plan. Once inside, we set up the protective barrier immediately."

George swallowed hard, steadying his nerves. "No turning back now."

With bated breath, they entered the west wing. A bone-chilling cold enveloped them, accompanied by an oppressive stillness. This was the lair of the vengeful spirit they had come to vanquish.

Khan hissed, his back arching. "It knows we're here. Get ready!"

Jessie and George exchanged a resolute glance. The final showdown was at hand.

Jessie, George, and Khan moved swiftly through the west wing, their footsteps echoing eerily in the cavernous space. Ancient artefacts and strange occult objects lined the walls and cluttered every surface. This had been Professor Langford's work area, the site of his ill-fated paranormal experiments.

Setting her jaw, Jessie unrolled the ancient Egyptian scroll onto a large table, weighing down the corners with small statues. George opened his bag and removed candles, herbs, and chalk. Khan stood alert, eyes darting, as if tracking invisible movements.

"Hurry," the cat warned. "The temperature's dropping fast."

Jessie and George worked in tandem, drawing intricate symbols on the floor while reciting the incantations detailed on the scroll. As they activated each section of the protective barrier, the symbols glowed an otherworldly blue. The temperature plummeted further, their breath coming out in icy plumes.

A bone-rattling roar shook the walls. The artefacts lining the shelves suddenly crashed to the floor. A dark, swirling mass manifested in the centre of the study, vaguely human in form.

Khan arched his back, spitting angrily. "It's here! The spirit knows what we intend to do!"

Jessie and George stood their ground inside the glowing barrier, faces set with determination. The final battle was upon them. They had to weaken the spirit before they could banish it for good.

Raising their voices in unison, they continued the incantation. The spirit screeched, "You cannot harm me, Sneferu." The screech echoed and reverberated throughout the mansion.

"This is the spirit of a Pharaoh, an ancient Egyptian king," Khan said.

Sneferu swooped toward them but met the crackling resistance of the barrier's energy. It battered the walls violently, making the whole room shake.

"Keep going!" Khan yowled over the din. "It's working!"

Jessie and George clasped hands, reciting the words that would save lives and Montague Mansion. The fate of the house and all in it depended on them now.

Jessie and George clung to each other inside the protective barrier, voices growing hoarse as they continued the endless chant. The temperature plummeted further, their breath freezing into icy clouds.

The vengeful spirit of Sneferu battered against their barrier, screeching and howling as it sought to break through. The study walls cracked under the onslaught. Ancient artefacts and books crashed to the floor, shattered beyond repair.

Khan's fur stood on end, his eyes glowing an unearthly blue as he focused his energy. "Enough of this!" His voice echoed with power. "Release your hold on this place, lost soul. Be at peace!"

Sneferu turned on the cat, laughing malevolently. "Never!" it rasped. "I will have my revenge!" It swooped toward Khan, spectral claws outstretched.

Khan stood firm, magic crackling around him. As the spirit drove into him, he became enveloped in blue light. The two entities struggled, Khan using all his strength to contain the vengeful being.

"Hurry!" Khan called to Jessie and George. "I can't hold it for long!"

Jessie and George moved in sync, hands still clasped. They wove a complex illusion spell, ancient words tumbling from their lips. The study walls rippled, reality distorting around the struggling spirit.

It shrieked in confusion, distracted from Khan. He broke away, chest heaving from the effort. "Well done!"

The trio regrouped inside the barrier, resolute. The final battle was upon them. Together, they would banish the spirit once and for all.

Khan's eyes glowed brighter as he scanned the room, sensing vulnerabilities only he could perceive. "The cursed artefact we need is hidden behind that bookcase," he said, flicking his tail toward the far wall.

Jessie and George hurried over. With a baffled glance in Khan's direction, their unspoken question was answered when Khan telekinetically slid the heavy oak bookcase aside, revealing a small alcove. Inside rested an ancient Egyptian sarcophagus, hieroglyphics etched into its surface.

"That's it!" Jessie said. She reached in and reverently lifted the sarcophagus lid. Nestled within was an amulet shaped like an ankh, the stone scarab at its centre pulsing with malevolent energy.

George carefully removed the amulet while Jessie replaced the lid. "Let's end this," he said, voice hard with determination.

The trio returned to the circle. As Jessie and George began the counter-curse, the spirit attacked with renewed fury. The study shook, books and artefacts crashing down. The walls cracked, plaster raining down.

Khan wove a shield around them, straining against the onslaught. "Hurry!" he urged through gritted teeth.

Jessie slipped the amulet around her neck, the stone scarab cold against her skin. Ancient Egyptian flowed from her lips as she and George completed the ritual. The amulet flared, amplifying their power tenfold.

The spirit of Sneferu shrieked, writhing in agony as the counter-curse hit it full force. But Jessie, George, and Khan stood strong, resolute in their purpose. With a final burst of energy, the spirit dissolved into wisps of shadow.

Silence fell. Jessie, George, and Khan slumped in exhaustion and relief. They had broken the curse and banished the spirit. Together, they had succeeded.

Jessie slowly got to her feet, feeling drained but triumphant. The confrontation with the vengeful spirit had pushed them all to their limits, but they had emerged victorious.

She looked over at George, who was leaning against a bookshelf catching his breath. His shirt was torn and there was a cut above his eyebrow, but his eyes shone with exhilaration.

"We did it," Jessie said, a weary smile spreading across her face. "I can't believe we actually did it."

George let out a small laugh. "I had my doubts there for a minute, but we pulled through." He reached down to scratch Khan behind the ears. "Thanks to this furball's quick thinking."

Khan purred, pleased by the praise but too tired to offer one of his usual witty retorts. The magical effort had taken a lot out of the mystical cat.

Jessie gazed around the study. The walls were still cracked and books were strewn everywhere, but the oppressive supernatural energy that had permeated the mansion was gone. The vengeful spirit's hold had been broken.

"I suppose we should go check on Lady Evelyn and the others," Jessie said after a moment. "They'll want to know it's safe to come out now."

George nodded and pushed himself away from the bookshelf with a groan. "Let's just hope they didn't completely trash the place while they were hiding from the spooky spectre."

Jessie laughed, linking her arm through George's as they headed for the study door, Khan trailing behind them. The mystery was solved, the day saved. And while their bodies ached, their spirits soared.

As Jessie, George, and Khan stepped out into the hallway, the rest of the mansion remained eerily quiet. The oppressive energy that had permeated the air was gone, replaced by an almost peaceful stillness.

Jessie called out, "Lady Evelyn? It's alright, you can come out now. The spirit is gone."

At first there was no response, then a door creaked open down the hall. Lady Evelyn's head poked out hesitantly. When she saw the trio standing there unharmed, relief flooded her face.

"Oh, thank heavens! I was worried sick about you all." She hurried over to them, the other guests cautiously emerging from various hiding spots to join her.

"You did it then? The curse has been lifted?" Lady Evelyn asked.

George nodded. "It wasn't easy, but we managed to banish the spirit for good."

Khan let out a celebratory meow and wound between Lady Evelyn's legs. She smiled and bent down to scratch his head affectionately.

"However can I repay you for what you've done? You've saved my life and so many others."

Jessie waved a hand. "No payment necessary. We were happy to help."

"Speak for yourself," George muttered with a wink. "I wouldn't say no to a generous bonus."

Jessie elbowed him in the ribs, but Lady Evelyn just laughed. "Of course, of course! Now, I believe some tea and relaxation is in order while I have the staff organise the repairs."

Linking her arm through Jessie's, Lady Evelyn led the way towards the parlour, the other guests chattering excitedly behind them, eager to hear every detail of the triumph over the vengeful spirit.

George, and Khan followed Lady Evelyn into the parlour, the warm glow of the fireplace and smell of freshly brewed tea helping to further ease their frayed nerves after the intense confrontation with the spirit.

As they settled into the plush chairs, Jessie let out a long exhale, the adrenaline still coursing through her system. She caught George's eye and they exchanged a knowing look - they had survived yet another brush with the paranormal, and once again made it out intact.

Khan leapt up into Jessie's lap, purring contentedly as she stroked his fur. She scratched behind his ears and murmured, "We make quite the team, don't we?" The cat blinked up at her in agreement.

George leaned back in his chair, stretching his long legs towards the fire. "All in a day's work, I'd say, though that spirit definitely packed a punch. Remind me not to anger any more ancient Egyptian souls."

Jessie nodded, gazing thoughtfully into the dancing flames. "We took some big risks in there... but it was worth it to help these people."

Though neither one was prone to sentimentality, they both recognised that they had formed a strong bond over the course of their adventures together - a bond forged in trust, teamwork, and no small amount of peril.

Khan's steady purring served as a soothing reminder that they had made it through unscathed. Jessie met George's eyes again and knew he understood - they had walked side by side into the face of danger and emerged victorious. Together, they were an unstoppable force against the forces of evil.

Jessie gently set Khan down and stood, smoothing out her skirt. "Well, I suppose we should be on our way. Lady Evelyn and her guests will want to settle back into their home now that it's free of that wretched spirit."

George nodded and rose as well. "Quite right. And we have that book auction to get to in the morning. Some rare grimoires that I think you'll find fascinating."

Jessie's eyes lit up at the prospect. She did love expanding her collection of mystical tomes. A trip to the book auction sounded like the perfect way to unwind after banishing a vengeful ghost.

As they gathered their belongings and made their way downstairs, Jessie took one last look around the grand mansion. The energy felt lighter now - the ominous chill had departed along with the spirit they had vanquished.

Lady Evelyn, her relatives, and the other guests were chatting brightly in the parlour, the atmosphere one of celebration and relief. Jessie was happy they had been able to restore peace to this stately home.

Stepping out into the cool night air, Jessie took a deep breath. The stars twinkled brightly above them as she, George, and Khan walked down the gravel driveway to where their car waited.

"So where to next?" George asked as he slid into the driver's seat. "I heard rumours of a haunted lighthouse up the coast near Southport. Could be our next case."

Jessie grinned, her mind already racing with possibilities. "Sounds intriguing. But first, let's find a cosy inn and get some rest. These old bones need a bit of recovery time."

George chuckled knowingly as Khan leapt up onto Jessie's lap, ready for their next adventure. The engine purred to life, and they drove off into the night, leaving the looming mansion behind. Wherever the paranormal called, the three of them would answer together.

Nineteen

It was....

Our investigators having banished the spirit of Sneferu, knew there were still parts of the investigation to bring to a conclusion.

Jessie swept into the drawing room, her auburn hair trailing behind her like a fiery comet. George and Khan flanked her on either side, their expressions grim.

"Thank you all for gathering here today," Jessie announced, meeting the nervous gazes of the suspects one by one. Some were relatives and some were staff or servants as Lady Montague would call them.

Mr Thompson, the gardener, shifted uneasily in his seat. Jessie's piercing hazel eyes settled on him, and he recoiled as if struck.

Jessie's gaze rapidly shifted to Penelope Montague who started fidgeting furiously with the hem of her shawl.

Then Jessie addressed the gathering.

"Charles Montague, the second murder victim," Jessie said sharply, "though I am loath to speak ill of the dead, he had a devious plan regarding Lady Evelyn's finances. He also blamed Mr Baxter of being complicit but we know that wasn't true, don't we Penelope?"

Penelope Montague squirmed, dabbing her brow with a handkerchief. "Surely you can't be serious! I had nothing to do with any of this!"

Khan arched his back and hissed, the fur on his spine standing on end. Jessie nodded at the cat appreciatively before turning her attention back to Penelope.

"I know you were involved in Professor Langford's death. And that of Charles Montague."

"This is preposterous," Penelope shrieked. "Why would I do such terrible things?"

"I am not accusing you of committing the acts of murder but you were involved in the planning and you know who actually killed the professor and your cousin, Charles, don't you?"

"I know nothing of the sort," Penelope snorted.

"Well, let's try this another way," George said gently, "does Mr Thompson smoke a pipe?"

Looking flustered, Penelope muttered, "I believe he does."

Holding up a piece of paper, George said, "And you know full well he smokes Craven Mixture, yes?"

"No."

"Well, please explain this receipt issued by the village shop to you after you bought a tin of Craven Mixture? Please answer carefully because we also have a witness statement from the shopkeeper," George said.

"Oh, very well then. It's not illegal to buy tobacco," Penelope said.

"No, it isn't you're right but why keep it a secret? Let's stop playing this game. You bought this tobacco for Mr Thompson, the gardener, didn't you?" George said.

"What if I did."

"You led Thompson to believe you loved him," Jessie said, taking over the reins from George.

"Nonsense. He's a servant and much older than me."

"So, tell us this, why did Amelia, the maid, see you two in an embrace?"

"She must have been... mistaken," Penelope muttered.

"You hatched a plan with the gardener after you duped him into thinking you cared for him. You wanted a share of the inheritance with hundreds of thousands of pounds. You schemed with Charles to kill the professor and send the death threats to Lady Evelyn hoping she would suffer a heart attack and die. Charles blamed Baxter to keep you out of it. It wasn't Baxter who paid some ruffian to write those ghastly letters. It was you. You paid Thompson.

It was Thompson who murdered Professor Langford and Charles Montague after he grew impatient waiting for his share of the ill-gotten gains."

"Nice theories, Miss Harper, but you have no evidence that I killed anyone," Thompson piped up from the back of the room.

"We will see about that, Mr Thompson, or should I say Mr Tanner, Francis Tanner, who changed his name to Thompson by deed poll after his third conviction as a cat burglar." Jessie said.

"This is how you did it. You unlocked Langford's study on the first floor as usual, locked the door behind you leaving the old worn key in the lock, killed the professor, left through the window, climbed down ladders you had left there in the night, but before leaving the room slipped the window latch shut using a piece of strong wire. You then returned the ladders and the wire to the shed.

You entered Charles Montague's room using the same method but this killing was more personal. Penelope had told you of their plan to get their share of Lady Evelyn's inheritance. You had felt let down by Charles Montague and grew impatient waiting for their plan to work so you took matters into your own hands."

"I don't have to put up with this rubbish," the gardener said.

"Your bumbling denial speaks volumes, Francis or do you prefer Frank?" Jessie said coolly. "You've been evasive since the moment we first clapped eyes on you. The ladder left indentations in the soft earth and that told us everything – and we retrieved the wire in your shed bearing the same paint marks that will undoubtedly match the paint and the marks on the window latch of the room where Langford was murdered."

Thompson leapt to his feet, knocking over his chair. "Lies! All lies! I'll not stand here and be insulted by you toffs!" He made for the door but stumbled over his fallen chair. Khan darted in front of him, blocking his path.

"Not so fast!" George said, grabbing Thompson by the arm. "We're not finished with you yet."

Thompson wrenched his arm away, breathing heavily. Jessie watched him, her expression unreadable. She doubted she had cracked tougher cases than this, and Thompson's unravelling only steeled her resolve. With George and Khan by her side, they would uncover the truth - no matter the cost.

Jessie stared Thompson down, her hazel eyes flashing. "Did you really think you could get away with it?" she asked quietly. "That we wouldn't put the pieces together?"

Thompson said nothing, glancing around the room wildly as if looking for an escape route.

Trapped, Thompson sank into a chair, all arrogance gone. "You don't understand," he whispered. "Penelope... she said she loved me... I did it for her."

Khan hissed again, his fur on end. Jessie's expression was icy. "At the cost of innocent lives? There's no excuse for what you've done."

Thompson buried his face in his hands. The evidence was overwhelming. All his scheming, all his duplicity had come to nothing. Jessie and George had outwitted him at every turn.

It was over.

Thompson leapt up, a mad glint in his eye. "You think you've won?" he snarled. "I won't go down without a fight!"

He snatched an ancient spear off the wall, brandishing it at Jessie and George. Khan arched his back, hissing menacingly.

"Khan, now!" Jessie yelled. The cat's eyes glowed bright as he summoned his magical energy. The spear flew from Thompson's grasp, clattering to the floor. Thompson cried out as ghostly ropes bound his wrists and ankles.

"It's over, Thompson," George said firmly. "There's nowhere left to run."

Thompson struggled against his bonds as heavy footsteps sounded down the hall. Three policemen entered the room, by pre-arrangement after Jessie and George had informed Bill Roberts of the time and place of the final showdown or dénouement as Bill called it.

"No! I was so close!" Thompson shouted as two of the policemen grabbed his arms. "That money should have been mine!"

Jessie stepped forward, meeting his wild eyes. "You are now one step closer to the gallows," she said calmly. Thompson glared at her with impotent rage as he was led away.

He failed to notice the third police officer, a woman constable, escorting Penelope out of the mansion by another door.

Finally, it was done. Jessie let out a long breath, the tension leaving her body. She bent to scratch Khan behind the ears. "We did it, boy," she murmured. The cat purred proudly.

Jessie leaned into George as they watched Thompson and Penelope Montague being led away in handcuffs, his angry shouts echoing down the hall. Penelope was silent and hanging her head in shame. Jessie felt a swell of emotions - sadness, anger, relief.

"I can't believe Thompson didn't see through Penelope," Jessie said quietly. "Kill all those innocent people because he was besotted with her."

George shook his head, his jaw set. "I know. But initially we didn't either. Anyway, we stopped him before he could hurt anyone else."

Determination flowed through Jessie, steadying her nerves. "Let's go tell the others," she said. "They deserve to know the truth too."

Hand in hand, Jessie and George returned to the drawing room where the remainder of the household were gathered. All eyes turned to them as they entered. Jessie saw fear, confusion, hope in their faces.

"It's over," George announced. "Mr Thompson, the gardener, not his real name by the way, has been arrested for the murders."

Shocked gasps and murmurs rippled through the room. Jessie stepped forward, holding up the evidence - the piece of wire, photographs of the matching marks on the window, and photographs of the tell-tale indentations left by the ladder in the soft earth.

"Thompson was infatuated with Penelope who frankly led him on so she could bend him to her will. Lady Evelyn's inheritance was at the root of these crimes. Thompson was simply a man obsessed," she explained. "He killed anyone who got in his way. But Penelope was a willing partner in planning these serious crimes."

Lady Evelyn swayed, putting a hand to her mouth. "Penelope, my own flesh and blood... I can't believe it."

Jessie went to her, squeezing her shoulder. "I'm so sorry. But it's the truth."

The others reacted with disbelief, anger, and grief. Jessie felt overwhelmed by the raw emotion in the room. But it was necessary for them to know. Penelope had deceived them all.

As Jessie and George comforted the group, Khan sat watching benevolently. Justice was done. The case was closed. For now.

Jessie took a deep breath as she prepared to have a private conversation with Lady Evelyn. This was the moment of truth, the turning point they had been working towards.

She met Lady Evelyn's eyes. "There's something you need to know about Penelope," she began gently. "We have evidence not only linking her directly to the murders but also to plotting with Charles to get their hands on your estate."

Lady Evelyn paled, shaking her head in disbelief. "No, it can't be. Penelope would never..."

"I'm afraid it's true." Jessie said.

"She was willing to kill for the money," Lady Evelyn whispered. "How could I not have known?"

Jessie squeezed her shoulder sympathetically. "She fooled us all."

At that moment a crash echoed from the hallway. Jessie and George exchanged alarmed looks.

"Thompson!" George exclaimed. "He's trying to escape!"

They rushed into the corridor just in time to see the gardener disappearing around a corner, a painting lying askew on the floor where he had knocked it over.

"After him!" Jessie shouted.

And the chase was on.

Jessie sprinted after Thompson as he fled through the mansion's winding halls and rooms. He knocked over chairs and vases, trying to slow their pursuit, but Jessie nimbly hurdled each obstacle.

"You won't get away with this, Thompson!" she yelled after him.

Just as they were gaining on him, Thompson dashed into the ballroom and slammed the double doors shut. Jessie threw her shoulders against the doors, but they barely budged.

"Khan!" Jessie called out urgently. "I need you!"

With a crackle of magic, the spectral cat appeared before her. His eyes flashed as he assessed the situation. With a flick of his tail, the doors flew open.

Thompson stood frozen at the balcony doors, realising he was trapped. Before he could react, Khan cast a spell over the doors, sealing them shut.

"It's over, Thompson," George said grimly. "There's nowhere left to run."

Panicking, Thompson grabbed a sword from a display on the wall and brandished it wildly. "Stay back! I'll kill you all!"

Jessie held up a pacifying hand. "Put down the sword. Let's talk about this."

As she spoke, Khan subtly used his powers to loosen Thompson's grip on the hilt. With a final magical tug, the sword went flying across the room.

Disarmed and defeated, Thompson fell to his knees. "I didn't want to hurt anyone," he sobbed. "This family, Penelope, made me do it!"

Jessie felt no pity but steeled herself. "You still have to face justice."

At that moment, the two embarrassed police men arrived. Having slipped his handcuffs once, they tightened a new pair until Thompson winced. "Serves you right," one said gruffly.

As Thompson was led away in handcuffs again, Jessie slipped an arm around George's waist.

"We make a pretty good team," she said with a tired smile.

George pulled her close. "That we do. What an adventure this has been!"

Khan twined between their legs, purring in agreement. The case was closed, but their work together had only just begun.

Jessie sank onto the sofa, exhausted but deeply satisfied. It had been a long, difficult case, but Thompson's arrest brought a sense of closure and justice.

George sat beside her, absently stroking Khan as the cat curled up on his lap. "I can't believe it's over," he murmured. "Part of me will miss the thrill of the chase."

Jessie nudged him playfully. "Knowing you, we'll stumble into another mystery before long."

"With Khan's help, no doubt," George said with a chuckle. The little cat purred proudly.

Jessie gazed out the window at the darkening sky. It had been a journey full of twists and turns, but they had weathered the challenges together. She knew without a doubt that George was the partner she wanted by her side.

Reaching out, she took his hand and gave it a squeeze. George looked at her, understanding in his eyes. No words were needed. The bond they shared went beyond the chaos of the last few days.

Khan glanced between them, sage as always. Jessie scratched under his chin. "What do you say, partner? Ready for a new adventure?"

The cat blinked slowly, as if to say... always. Tomorrow would bring new mysteries, but tonight, they had earned a moment of peace.

Later that evening, as Jessie drifted off to sleep, visions of future cases danced in her head. She saw herself and George exploring a haunted lighthouse, tracking down stolen jewels, and foiling art forgers. With Khan's magic and intellect on their side, they would be an unstoppable team. The world had no shortage of puzzles to solve, and she couldn't wait to unravel them together. For now, rest. But tomorrow... tomorrow brought promise of intrigue yet to come.

Twenty

A Gift

ONCE MORE IN THE sanctuary of their makeshift office at the mansion, Jessie sank into the plush armchair, absent-mindedly stroking Khan as he purred in her lap. George leaned against the mahogany desk, arms crossed, gazing thoughtfully at the floor.

"Well, that was certainly a close call," Jessie said, breaking the silence. "If it wasn't for Khan's intervention, Thompson might've gotten away for good."

George nodded. "Just barely stopped him before he made it to those secret passages. Good thing Khan foiled him." He smiled at the cat, who blinked lazily back at him.

"We make quite the team, don't we?" Jessie said. "Who would've thought a couple of bookish types like us would get tangled up in such a thrilling caper."

"With a paranormal twist to boot," George added wryly.

Just then, the study doors burst open, and Lady Evelyn swept into the room, the silk train of her evening gown trailing behind her.

"My dears, I can't thank you enough for everything you've done," she gushed, clasping her hands together. "If it weren't for your courage and determination, I shudder to think what that horrid man might have done to me, or any of my friends."

Jessie reddened slightly. "Really, we were just doing our duty, Lady Evelyn. We're so pleased we could be of service."

"Oh, don't be so modest!" Lady Evelyn cried. "Why, you're the most brilliant detectives I've ever had the pleasure of meeting. The way you followed every clue, even delving into the paranormal... it was extraordinary!"

Khan gave a proud meow from Jessie's lap. She stroked his back, sharing a knowing look with George. No matter what mysteries came next, they'd be ready to solve them together.

Jessie smiled modestly at Lady Evelyn's effusive praise. "You're too kind, my lady. We were happy to lend our talents to help solve this mystery and bring the gardener and Penelope to justice."

George nodded in agreement. "Aye, 'twas our duty and our honour. Your faith in us is thanks enough."

But Lady Evelyn would have none of their humility. "Nonsense! Your work deserves a proper reward. Please, accept this small token of my gratitude."

She retrieved a lacquered box from her desk and presented it to Jessie and George with an elegant flourish. Jessie's eyes widened as she opened the lid to reveal an exquisite jade pendant on a golden chain.

"My lady, this is too generous," Jessie breathed, admiring the pendant's intricate carvings.

"Not at all," Lady Evelyn insisted. "It pales in comparison to what I owe you both." She turned her warm gaze to Khan. "And you, Sir Khan. What adventures you've led us all on! Never have I encountered a more extraordinary feline."

Khan blinked his green eyes slowly, as if to say he expected no less. Jessie laughed and stroked his inky fur.

"We shall continue to be in your debt," Lady Evelyn finished earnestly. "Should you ever require my assistance, you need only ask. I'll leave you alone now."

Before Lady Evelyn left, Jessie and George thanked her sincerely, overcome by her generosity. As Jessie clasped the pendant around her neck, she shared a knowing look with George. Though the mystery was solved, their adventures were only just beginning.

Jessie's fingers brushed against George's as they both grasped the ornate box containing Lady Evelyn's gift. She felt a spark shoot up her arm at the contact. Their eyes met and Jessie noticed George's cheeks flush ever so slightly.

In that moment, everything clicked into place. The shared glances, racing hearts, and unspoken words over the past weeks suddenly made sense. Jessie realized, with crystal clarity, that her feelings for George had developed into something far deeper than partnership or friendship.

George held Jessie's gaze, seeming to read the recognition in her eyes. She could tell he felt the shift between them too. His shoulders relaxed and he offered her a small, hopeful smile.

Emboldened by the revelation, Jessie gathered her courage. She took a step closer to George, never breaking eye contact. "George, I... I need to tell you something. Over these last few weeks, I've come to care for you a great deal. More than I ever expected."

She paused, heartbeat thundering in her ears. "You've become so important to me. I don't know what the future holds, but I know I want to face it together, with you by my side."

Jessie held her breath, terrified but also exhilarated by her confession. She searched George's face for a reaction, hoping against hope she hadn't misunderstood.

George's eyes widened at Jessie's heartfelt words. He opened his mouth to speak, but no sound came out at first. Jessie could see the emotions playing across his face - surprise, hesitation, and finally acceptance.

"Jessie..." he began, his voice soft. "I won't deny that I've been struggling with my feelings. When we first started working together, I never imagined we could be more than colleagues."

He gently took her hands in his, interlocking their fingers. "But over time, I've come to rely on you. Not just your skills, but your kindness, your humour, your strength. You've become so special to me."

George's thumbs caressed the backs of her hands as he gathered the courage to continue. "I was afraid to acknowledge it, but you're right. What we have now means everything. I want to face the future together too, Jessie."

At his words, Jessie's anxieties melted away. Joy and relief flooded through her as she squeezed George's hands. They shared a long look, a thousand unspoken sentiments passing between them.

Then, drawn together like magnets, they embraced. Jessie rested her head on George's shoulder, his arms encircling her waist. She could hear his racing heartbeat as they held each other close.

In this perfect moment, the world fell away. The only thing that mattered was their connection. Whatever mysteries lay ahead, they would face them together.

Jessie and George remained locked in a tender embrace, lost in their shared feelings of affection and newfound commitment. A subtle purring sound broke the silence, and they turned to see Khan observing them with knowing eyes.

The mystical black cat wore an expression of pure satisfaction, as if he had been expecting this development all along. His purrs grew louder and his tail swished back and forth lazily as he padded over to the couple.

"Well, it's about time, you two," Khan remarked in his deep, velvety voice. "I was beginning to wonder if I'd have to intervene with a love potion or two."

Jessie laughed as she reached down to scratch behind Khan's ears. "Oh, so you're taking credit now?" she teased.

Khan arched into her hand, his rumbling purr intensifying. "I can't help being an excellent matchmaker. Though in truth, you both simply needed a nudge in the right direction."

"We're grateful for your wisdom, as always," George said sincerely, nodding to the cat.

Just then, Lady Evelyn re-entered the study. Her face lit up when she saw Jessie and George standing together holding hands with Khan contentedly purring at their feet.

"My dears, I'm delighted to see you've finally acknowledged what was clear to me from the start," Lady Evelyn said warmly. She clasped her hands together in joy. "You two make such a perfect team, in every way. With courage and compassion on your side, you are unstoppable."

Jessie and George thanked Lady Evelyn for her kind words and support. As they all shared a celebratory toast together, the future seemed brighter than ever.

Jessie and George smiled at each other, their hands still intertwined. After everything they had been through together, this moment felt like a new beginning.

"I know our work is far from over," Jessie said, meeting George's gaze. "There will always be mysteries to unravel and wrongs to right. But now we have each other."

George nodded, his thumb gently caressing Jessie's hand. "Together we're stronger," he agreed. "I've never been more certain of anything."

Khan let out a soft meow, as if in agreement. The cat's wise eyes seemed to say he would support them no matter where their journey led next.

Lady Evelyn regarded the trio fondly. "Go forward with courage and purpose," she encouraged them. "And know you will always have a home here should you need it. Enough of this old woman's advice. I must go back to my friends or they will think I have been kidnapped." Jessie and George thanked her sincerely. She smiled kindly as she left the room.

Then alone again, with one final smile exchanged between them, their lips met in a passionate kiss. It was a promise, a seal upon their bond. They parted slowly, foreheads touching. The future lay ahead of them, full of mystery, but they would face it hand in hand.

Khan purred in satisfaction and trotted ahead toward the study door. Jessie and George followed, ready for whatever adventure awaited them next.

Twenty-One
EPILOGUE

ON THEIR RETURN TO Liverpool, Jessie and George were thinking of their last moments at Montague Mansion.

The final echoes of Lady Evelyn's laughter filled the room as all present shared a well-deserved toast, having successfully solved the mystery of the curse that had plagued Montague Mansion and its occupants for weeks. The relief in Lady Evelyn's eyes was palpable, and her grateful friends showered the duo with compliments, their admiration adding to the warm glow that surrounded Jessie and George.

"Here's to us," George said, raising his glass to meet Jessie's, the clink of crystal punctuating the end of one adventure and the beginning of another.

"Here's to us," Jessie agreed, taking a sip of her champagne, feeling the bubbles tickle her nose as the warmth in her chest spread, fuelled not only by their recent success but also by the undeniable connection she shared with George.

Their partnership had blossomed from an unlikely pairing into a formidable team, and it was with a sense of pride that they returned to their agency office in Dale Street in the heart of bustling Liverpool, ready to take on new challenges and mysteries. As they stepped inside, the familiar scent of old books and leather-bound journals welcomed them, a testament to Jessie's past as a librarian and the foundation of her expertise in the paranormal.

"Word certainly spreads fast in this city, doesn't it?" George remarked as he hung up his coat, gesturing to the congratulatory notes and telegrams that had arrived while they were away. "I suppose solving a cursed mystery does wonders for one's reputation."

"Indeed," Jessie replied, a hint of amusement in her voice. "It seems our little agency has become quite the talk of Liverpool." She picked up one of the messages, scanning its contents before placing it back on the pile. "We've already received several inquiries about potential new cases."

"Then I'd say we've earned ourselves a moment to celebrate our achievements," George said, moving closer to

Jessie. "After all, we make a rather exceptional team, don't you think?"

"Exceptional indeed," Jessie agreed, her hazel eyes meeting George's gaze. "And if this recent case is any indication, we'll only continue to grow stronger and more skilled at solving mysteries together."

"Cheers to that," George replied, his smile mirroring Jessie's as they both took a moment to bask in the glow of their shared success. Little did they know that this was just the beginning, and the city of Liverpool had many more secrets waiting to be uncovered.

As Jessie and George stood in their agency, they couldn't help but feel a sense of pride at the recent success that had placed them on the map. They exchanged glances, both knowing that their lives were about to change for the better. Just then, a languid stretch caught their attention, and they found Khan sprawled across the desk, his green eyes fixed on the pair with an air of superiority.

"Ah, there's our trusted sidekick," George said, chuckling as he approached the feline. "I suppose you're here to claim your share of the credit, eh, Khan?"

Khan flicked his tail and emitted a low, rumbling purr, as if acknowledging the praise. Jessie grinned and added, "Well, we can't deny that your magical abilities have been invaluable in solving our cases."

"Indeed," George agreed, leaning down to stroke Khan's fur. "Without your assistance, we wouldn't be where we are today."

"Meow," Khan replied, feigning disinterest despite the faint hint of satisfaction in his eyes.

At that moment, the office telephone rang. "Yes, Isabel, send him in," George said.

The office door opened, and a well-dressed gentleman entered, carrying a briefcase. He looked around nervously before spotting Jessie and George, who immediately turned their attention to him.

"Are you Miss Harper and Mr Jenkins?" the man asked, his voice trembling slightly.

"Indeed, we are," Jessie replied, stepping forward with a warm smile. "How may we help you?"

"My name is John Carruthers. I've heard about your recent success in solving that cursed mystery at Montague Mansion," the man explained, clearly impressed by their reputation. "I have a case of my own that I'd like to entrust to you."

"Of course," George interjected, all traces of humour gone as he shifted into professional mode. "Please, have a seat, and tell us everything."

"Thank you," the man said, visibly relieved as he settled into a chair and began to relay the details of his case.

As Jessie and George listened intently to their new client, Khan observed from his perch on the desk, a glint in his eyes that suggested he was already anticipating the next mystery. And though the challenges ahead were sure to be demanding, Jessie, George, and Khan were more than ready to face them together, propelled by their newfound success and their unshakeable bond.

Having agreed a small fee with the man to carry out a preliminary investigation, Jessie and George drove to Mr Carruthers' home at Crosby. At his suggestion, the pair climbed into the attic.

The attic was dimly lit, dust particles dancing in the few beams of sunlight that filtered through the small window. Jessie and George stood side by side, examining a set of peculiar symbols etched into the floorboards. Swirls and lines intertwined, forming an intricate pattern that seemed to pulsate with energy.

"Jessie, do you recognise these markings?" George asked, his brow furrowed in concentration.

"Actually, I think they might be connected to an ancient druidic ritual," Jessie replied thoughtfully, her hazel eyes narrowing as she traced one of the swirling lines with her finger. "But I'll need to consult my books back at the office to be sure."

"Of course," George said, nodding supportively. He took out his trusty magnifying glass and began to carefully inspect the symbols, making notes in a small leather-bound notebook.

Khan throwing off his cloak of invisibility, appeared next to Jessie and George. "Your human knowledge is so limited," Khan remarked, his tone dripping with condescension. "I could solve this in a jiffy if I were so inclined."

"Ah, but where's the fun in that, Khan?" Jessie quipped, a smile tugging at the corners of her mouth. "Besides, we wouldn't want to deprive you of the chance to mock us for our ignorance, now, would we?"

"Indeed not," Khan purred, his green eyes glinting with amusement before he disappeared once more. Preliminary investigation over, Jessie and George drove back to Dale Street.

As Jessie delved into her research, George continued his methodical examination of the notes he had made of the scene. The two worked in harmony, each trusting the other's expertise and instincts implicitly. It was this seamless teamwork that had made them such a formidable duo in solving mysteries.

However, as the investigation progressed, it became apparent that their newfound romance added a layer of complexity to their partnership. They found themselves stealing glances at each other, smiling shyly when their eyes met. It was a delicate dance, trying to balance their professional relationship with the blossoming feelings that threatened to consume them.

"George," Jessie began hesitantly one evening as they sat in their office, surrounded by stacks of books and papers. "Do you think... can we truly make this work? Being both partners in crime-solving and... well, partners in life?"

"I've been wondering the same thing, Jessie," George admitted, his dark eyes searching her face earnestly. "But I believe in us. We've faced so many challenges together already. Surely we can navigate through this as well."

"True," Jessie mused, her heart swelling with affection for the man who had become her closest confidant. "We must simply remember to communicate openly and honestly, even when it's difficult."

"Agreed," George said, reaching for her hand and giving it a gentle squeeze. "Together, there's nothing we can't overcome."

"Ahem," Khan interjected, feigning disinterest as he groomed his paw. "I hate to interrupt this touching display of sentimentality, but perhaps we could return to the matter at hand?"

"Of course, Khan," Jessie replied, rolling her eyes affectionately at their feline companion. "Back to work it is."

And so, armed with trust, love, and a healthy dose of sarcasm from their enigmatic cat, Jessie Harper and George Jenkins continued their quest to unravel the mysteries that awaited them.

As Jessie sat in the cosy corner of their office, her eyes drifted to the window where raindrops playfully raced one another down the pane. She glanced over at George, who was intently studying a map of the city spread out before him on the desk. Her heart swelled with affection for the man who had become not only her partner in crime-solving but also in life. The soft patter of rain mixed with the crackle of the fire served as a soothing backdrop to their conversation.

"George," she began, breaking the silence. "We've come so far since we first met, haven't we?"

He looked up from the map and met her gaze with a warm smile. "Indeed, we have. I couldn't have imagined back then that we would be running our own successful agency together."

"Nor could I have predicted how... fond I would grow of you," Jessie said softly, a light blush creeping across her cheeks.

"Neither did I," George replied, his voice filled with emotion. "Jessie, I want you to know that I am committed to our partnership, both professionally and personally. I believe we can make a real difference in this city, solving mysteries and helping those in need."

"Thank you, George," Jessie whispered, touched by his words. "I feel the same way. Together, we can face whatever challenges come our way."

Just as they shared a tender smile, the telephone rang shrilly, jarring them back to reality. George answered the call, his expression becoming more serious as he listened to the person on the other end. After hanging up, he turned to Jessie, excitement sparkling in his eyes.

"Jessie, that was Mrs Hennessey, our last client before we took in the Montague Mansion case. We've cracked the case! The missing heirloom has been found, and it turns out the butler was behind the theft all along just as I said."

"Really?" Jessie exclaimed, her eyes wide with surprise. "I never would have suspected him!"

"Neither did I, initially," George admitted. "But our intuition has greatly improved since our first case. We've learned to trust each other's instincts and follow leads that might have once seemed far-fetched."

"Indeed," Jessie agreed.

George added, "And it seems our reputation is growing. Our client was beyond grateful for our help and even mentioned recommending us to some of her well-connected friends."

"Excellent news!" Jessie exclaimed. "It appears we can look forward to many more interesting cases in our future."

As they basked in the glow of their recent successes, Khan sauntered over, tail flicking proudly as he took his place on the windowsill. "Well, well, another mystery solved thanks to my keen feline senses, of course," he quipped, a smug grin evident in his green eyes.

"Of course, Khan," Jessie replied with a chuckle. "Where would we be without your invaluable assistance?"

"Wallowing in a sea of mediocrity, no doubt," Khan retorted, preening under the praise.

Jessie exchanged an amused glance with George, both marvelling at their extraordinary cat and the unique bond they all shared. Together, they faced an exciting future filled with mysteries, challenges, and love – a future they couldn't wait to embrace.

Jessie gazed out the window of their humble agency office once more, watching the sun cast its warm golden rays across Liverpool's bustling streets now that the rain had ceased. She sighed contentedly, her thoughts drifting back to their first meetings in the Kardomah coffee house, when George met her just after the death of her friend, Elsie, than later to set out his future plans and invite her to be his business partner in the fledgling Dale Street Private Investigations Agency.

"Hard to believe it all started over a cup of coffee," George mused, apparently following her train of thought. He leaned against the windowsill, his strong arms folded across his chest.

"Indeed," Jessie agreed, her hazel eyes sparkling as she turned to face him. "You were so desperate for help, and I happened to be in the right place at the right time."

"More like fate brought us together," George corrected, his voice softening. "Our partnership has grown stronger with each case, and our relationship... well, it's evolved into something quite extraordinary."

A tender smile graced Jessie's lips as she placed her hand on his. "I couldn't agree more, George. We've come a long way since that day, and I'm grateful for the growth we've experienced together."

"Ahem." The sudden sound of Khan clearing his throat interrupted their heartfelt conversation. The cat lounged on the desk nearby, his whiskers twitching with amusement. "As touching as this little trip down memory lane is, I think it's important to remember who the real star of this team is."

"Of course, Khan," Jessie replied, rolling her eyes playfully. "How could we forget your indispensable role in our investigations?"

"Indeed," George chimed in, his own eyes twinkling with humour. "Your magical abilities, not to mention your unparalleled wit, have been invaluable in solving our cases."

Khan puffed out his chest proudly, flicking his tail in satisfaction. "Well, it's about time someone acknowledged my contributions. You two would be lost without me."

"True," Jessie said, exchanging a knowing glance with George. "We wouldn't be where we are today without your help, Khan. And for that, we're eternally grateful."

As the trio basked in the warmth of their shared success and camaraderie, the anticipation of future mysteries and adventures filled the room, promising even greater growth and stronger bonds in the days to come.

In a restaurant in Liverpool's Adelphi hotel, the warm glow of candlelight flickered against the polished silverware and elegant china spread across the table, casting a cosy atmosphere over the celebratory dinner. Friends and clients alike including Lady Evelyn and many of her friends had gathered to honour Jessie, George, and Detective Sergeant Bill Roberts for their impressive work in solving cases and helping those in need.

"Here's to Jessie, George, and our dear friend Bill," Lady Evelyn proclaimed as she raised her wine glass, a bright smile lighting up her face. "Your dedication and brilliance have brought justice and resolution to so many lives. We are forever grateful."

"Cheers!" echoed the guests as they raised their glasses in unison, the sound of crystal clinking filling the room with a sense of joy and accomplishment.

Jessie felt her cheeks flush with pride as she exchanged a glance with George, who returned her gaze with a soft smile that made her heart swell. Beside them, Detective Sergeant Bill Roberts offered a humble nod, clearly touched by the outpouring of appreciation.

As the evening progressed, the group shared stories of their recent successes, laughter and camaraderie weaving through the conversations like a comforting thread. Jessie couldn't help but marvel at how far they had come since she and George first met, their relationship blossoming not only professionally but personally as well.

"Bill," George said, addressing his friend, "You've been an invaluable ally throughout our investigations. The support of the Liverpool police has played no small part in our achievements," George paused for thought then added, "that support also applies to the budding scientific team. They did some outstanding work on matching the samples from the window at the mansion to the wire found in Thompson's shed."

"Thank you, George" Bill replied, his voice tinged with emotion. "It's been an honour to work alongside such dedicated and talented individuals. You, Jessie, and that extraordinary cat of yours make quite the team." He chuckled, a twinkle in his eye. A twinkle that disguised he knew far more about Khan than he was prepared to divulge.

"Speaking of Khan," Jessie mused, scanning the room for their feline companion. She spotted him lounging near the kitchen doors, observing the festivities with his signature air of superiority. "I believe he's taking credit for most of our accomplishments."

"Ah, there he is!" George chuckled, raising his glass in Khan's direction. "To our magical and witty sidekick, who, if he could talk would never fail to remind us of his indispensable role in our investigations."

"Cheers to Khan!" echoed the guests, turning their attention to the cat, who flicked his tail in satisfaction, as if acknowledging their praise.

As the evening drew to a close, Jessie felt a deep sense of contentment and anticipation wash over her. The challenges they had faced together had only served to strengthen their bond, and she knew that more mysteries and adventures awaited them in the future.

"Tonight has been wonderful," Jessie whispered to George as they stood by the large restaurant window, moonlight streaming through the glass. "I can't help but feel excited for what lies ahead for us, both professionally and personally."

"Neither can I," George replied, his hand finding hers and giving it a gentle squeeze. "We've come so far, Jessie, and I have no doubt that we'll continue to grow and thrive together."

"Indeed," Jessie agreed, her eyes shining with optimism. "Whatever the future holds for us, I know that we'll face it united, with strength and determination."

And as they shared a tender smile, the promise of countless mysteries and challenges yet to be unravelled lay before them, an adventure waiting just beyond the horizon.

The last of the evening's laughter and applause faded as Jessie, George, and Khan found themselves alone in the restaurant. The warm glow from the fireplace cast a warm atmosphere in the room, while the lingering scent of cigar smoke and champagne hinted at the merriment that had just taken place.

"Another successful case," George remarked with a smile, his eyes twinkling in the firelight. "Our reputation has certainly grown since we first met."

"Indeed, it has," Jessie agreed, her gaze shifting to Khan who was perched atop a nearby chair. The enigmatic feline, with his uncanny ability to sense the paranormal, had been an invaluable asset in their investigations.

"Khan, you've outdone yourself this time," she said, her voice filled with admiration. "Your keen senses have once again proven to be indispensable."

Khan flicked his tail and looked down at them with an expression that seemed to say, 'Naturally, I'm always right.'

"Speaking of indispensable," George began, a playful grin on his face, "I think it's about time we made good on our promise to treat Khan to his favourite salmon dinner."

"Ah, yes," Jessie replied, chuckling. "I believe he's more than earned it."

As they prepared to leave the hotel, the faint sound of jazz music drifted in through the open window, a reminder of Liverpool's vibrant pulse in the 1930s. The bustling streets outside were alive with the energy of a city that never slept, a stark contrast to the quiet sanctum they currently shared.

"Jessie?" George called, breaking her reverie. "Are you ready?"

"Of course," she answered, giving him a warm smile before turning to Khan. "Shall we, Mr Feline Detective?"

With an air of nonchalance, Khan leaped off the chair and sauntered towards the door, leading the way as if to say, 'Well, it's about time. I'm hungry.'

As they followed Khan through the Liverpool streets, Jessie caught George's hand in hers, intertwining their fingers. She felt a sense of contentment wash over her, grateful for the adventures they had experienced together and eager for the challenges that lay ahead.

"George," she whispered, "I have a feeling our future will be filled with even more mysteries and excitement."

"Wouldn't have it any other way," he replied, squeezing her hand reassuringly.

With that, Jessie, George, and Khan continued into the night, ready to face whatever new challenges awaited them, united by their unbreakable bond and the joy they found in each other's company.

As they entered the Dale Street office. the sound of a ringing phone pierced the calm night air, echoing through the dimly lit streets of Liverpool. As Jessie, George, and Khan walked up the stairs, their shadows cast by the flickering streetlights outside, they couldn't help but feel a sense of anticipation for what awaited them on the other end of the line.

"Seems like our services are in demand tonight," Jessie mused, her hazel eyes sparkling with excitement.

"Indeed," George agreed, his grip on Jessie's hand tightening ever so slightly. "Let's hope it's a case worthy of our talents."

"Meow." Khan chimed in, his tail curling around Jessie's ankle as if to claim ownership of their shared destiny.

"Alright, Mr Feline Detective," Jessie laughed, disentangling herself from Khan's grasp. "Let's not get too ahead of ourselves."

"Dale Street Private Investigations, how may we help you?" Jessie answered, trying to keep her voice steady despite her heart racing in her chest.

"Ah, Miss Harper, I've heard quite a bit about your recent success with Lady Evelyn's case," the caller began, his voice rich and smooth like dark chocolate. "I have a rather peculiar situation that I believe requires your unique expertise."

"Go on," Jessie urged, glancing over at George and Khan, who were watching her intently.

"Very well," the mysterious man continued. "I'm afraid I cannot divulge too much over the telephone but suffice it to say that my home has become the centre of some rather...strange occurrences. If you and your partner would be so kind as to pay me a visit tomorrow, I can explain everything in person."

"Can you give us a hint of what we're dealing with?" Jessie asked, curiosity getting the better of her.

"Let's just say that there are forces at play that defy explanation," the man replied cryptically. "I look forward to our meeting, Miss Harper. Goodnight."

"Wait!" Jessie called, but it was too late – the line went dead, leaving an air of mystery hanging in the air.

"Jessie, what did he say?" George inquired, his brow furrowed with concern.

"Something about strange occurrences and unexplained forces," she replied, a shiver running down her spine. "It sounds like our next case might be just as challenging as the last one."

"Meow," Khan agreed, his green eyes gleaming with mischief.

"Here we go again," Jessie sighed, unable to suppress the thrill of excitement that pulsed through her veins.

"Salmon first," Khan said.

THE END

Acknowledgements

This book may not have been possible without the immense help I received from Jane Roberts from England and Michele from Georgia, USA, who alpha and beta read the first drafts in addition to making further suggestions when it reached the ARC stage.

Heartfelt thanks are also owed to my Cozy Review team They did a sterling job and made life much easier for me and my editor. As usual, I also thank my editor and my book cover designer, the lovely and talented Eeva who is the Book Khaleesi.

About KJ Cornwall

KJ CORNWALL IS THE pen name of Stephen Bentley, a former British police Detective Sergeant, pioneering Operation Julie undercover detective, and barrister. He now writes in the true crime and crime fiction genres and contributes occasionally to Huffington Post UK on undercover policing, and mental health issues.

He is possibly best known for his bestselling Operation Julie memoir and as co-author of Operation George: A Gripping True Crime Story of an Audacious Undercover Sting.

His Operation Julie book has been optioned and is in development as an 8-part TV series in addition to that huge and unique police operation being pitched to broadcasters as a documentary.

Stephen is a member of the UK's Society of Authors and the Crime Writers' Association.

For new releases and news about the Operation Julie TV series/documentary, you may wish to subscribe to Stephen's newsletter by downloading your free copy of Short Stories by a Tall Guy.

Stephen, with Dominic Smith, also writes as part of a writing team in the Undercover Legends series under the pen name of David Le Courageux.

Now a multi-genre author, Stephen also writes cozy mysteries in the pen name of KJ Cornwall.

You can listen to Stephen talking about his Operation Julie undercover days on the BBC Radio 4 Life Changing programme/podcast available 24/7 worldwide on BBC Sounds. And on the same platform, he also contributes to Acid Dream: The Great LSD Plot.

Sign up to the mailing list for news of books by Stephen and KJ Cornwall here[1].

---

1. Newsletterhttps://stephenbentley.eo.page/rz1db

Also By

You can find all books written by Stephen Bentley and his pen names including KJ Cornwall using the Booklinker images below or clicking here.

You can also buy his books direct here.

KJ Cornwall Books2Read page is here. Stephen Bentley Books2Read page is here.

Click the image for more details:

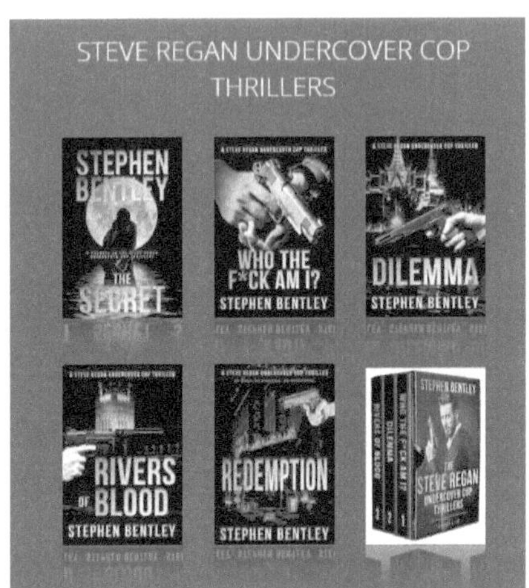

STEVE REGAN UNDERCOVER COP THRILLERS
STEPHEN BENTLEY
THE SECRET
WHO THE F*CK AM I?
STEPHEN BENTLEY
DILEMMA
STEPHEN BENTLEY
RIVERS OF BLOOD
STEPHEN BENTLEY
REDEMPTION
STEPHEN BENTLEY
STEPHEN BENTLEY
THE STEVE REGAN UNDERCOVER COP THRILLERS

Stephen Bentley
DETECTIVE MATT DEAL THRILLERS
MERCY
STEPHEN BENTLEY
MAYHEM
STEPHEN BENTLEY
MOBOCRACY
STEPHEN BENTLEY
MONTANA
STEPHEN BENTLEY
NIGHT'S REDEMPTION
STEPHEN BENTLEY

If you prefer to use QR codes you can find out more about all books written by KJ Cornwall and sign up for the mailing list by scanning the QR code below.

Similarly, you can find full details of true crime books and hard boiled thrillers written by Stephen Bentley by scanning the QR code below.